George Douglas

The Fireside Tragedy

George Douglas

The Fireside Tragedy

ISBN/EAN: 9783337249144

Printed in Europe, USA, Canada, Australia, Japan

Cover: Foto ©Andreas Hilbeck / pixelio.de

More available books at **www.hansebooks.com**

THE FIRESIDE TRAGEDY

THE FIRESIDE TRAGEDY

A Play

BY

SIR GEORGE DOUGLAS, BART.

EDINBURGH: DAVID DOUGLAS

1887

CONTENTS.

A

THE FIRESIDE TRAGEDY.

Characters.

MRS. MAR	. . .	*A Widow : Mistress of Windy Walls.*
WILLIAM LEE	. . .	*Her Son by her first marriage.*
CUTHBERT MAR	. .	*Her Son by her second marriage.*
ISABELLA	. . . .	*Her Niece.*
PLAYFAIR	. . . .	*Mrs. Mar's Steward.*
PRUDENCE	. .	*His Daughter.*
OLD HICKATHRIFT	. .	*A Pensioner on the Farm.*
JACK	. . . . .	*His Son : Husband to Prudence.*
SOLOMON MEIKLEJOHN	.	*A half-witted Hobbledyhoy.*
DAVY	. . . .	*Odd Man on the Farm.*
DERRICK LOBB }	. . .	*Officers of the Coastguard.*
A PEDLAR.		
HOB HOBNAIL SWINGTREE TOM TUCKER NICK FARTHING TIMOTHY }	. .	*Guests at the Christmas Party.*
A FIDDLER.		

NEIGHBOURS ; FARM SERVANTS *and their* WIVES *and* DAUGHTERS *assembled to keep Christmas at Windy Walls :*—GUIZARDS :— COASTGUARDSMEN.

Scene.

A Farm House on the Coast.

Costumes.

After the Rustics and Sailors in George Morland's Paintings, and the Woodcuts of Thomas Bewick.

THE FIRESIDE TRAGEDY.

ACT I.

SCENE: *The kitchen of an old-fashioned Farm House, in the style of the Interior in Sir David Wilkie's 'Blind Man's Buff.'—Three Doors ;—of which, L leads into the Supper-room ; R to other parts of the house ; and C out of doors.—A Screen.— The room is decorated with Evergreens and Mottoes for Christmas.—As the Curtain rises, DAVY is discovered mounted upon a Pair of Steps, in the act of hanging up a Mistletoe Bough; PLAYFAIR, with legs apart and arms akimbo, stands by, looking on.*

Davy. There! now I call that a pretty bough.

Play. As pretty a mistletoe bough, and so I'd wager, as any that hangs in house or hall to-night . . .

Davy (*coming down from Steps*). Between this and Lunnon !—I say, steward . . .

Play. Well, Davy?

Davy. Ye know, 'Christmas comes but once a year.'

Play. That's true !

Davy. Well, I've made up my mind to enjoy myself accordingly to-night !

Play. To enjoy thyself, lad? 'tis no more than right ye should;—and so, please God, will I too.   For, with vittles and drink such as be spread i' the next room, 'twould be flying i' the face of a bountiful Providence if any man should do less.—Why, man alive ! only think o' that noble shorthorn heifer—killed a' purpose that we might enjoy ourselves.

Davy. I believe 'ee.   And of the bee-u-tiful dairy-fed pork . . .

Play. The prime four-shear gimmers . . .

Davy. And the goose pies.

Play. Not to speak o' the turkeys, the black-puddens, and the sausages . . .

Davy. O steward ! you do make my mouth water.

Play. . . . The dumplin's and the mince pies.   And, last but not least, the pudding—and a glorious pudding 'a be ;—as big and as round as the head upon our snow man ; stuck as full of plums as a parson's plate wi' ha'pence on a Sunday ;—with a sprig o' holly i' the centre !

Davy. Tchk !

Play. And an ocean o' hot spiced ale to come after to wash un down.

Davy. Tchk!

Play. Ye may well smack your lips ; for there's meat an' drink there such as a man don't see every day—'pon my soul, it be fit to set before princes! And, my son, remember this, we be bound to do 'em justice—we be bound in good manners to do 'em justice !

Davy. Never fear but I shall do my share. I'll tell 'ee, Maister : there was some of us youngsters laid our heads together and agreed to take but a bite and a sup at breakfas'-time and to go without our dinners altogether—a' purpose to do 'em justice. And we've all been a-sliding on the duck-pond, keeping-the-pot-a-boiling, ever sin' four o'clock—all a' purpose to do 'em justice !

Play. Well done, well done ! it does me good to hear thee, lad ; for 'tis that's the proper spirit at Christmas-time. And when Christmas is no longer Christmas, 'twill be an ill day for the country at large ; and I hope that I for one may never live to see it !

[*Enter* PRUDENCE.]

Prue. Goodness ! father, is it possible ? gossiping here when the guests will be upon us afore we know where we are—and not as much as a stick prepared ! 'Tis allus the way ;—except I look to un with my own eyes, not a thing in this house can I get done. Now, for heaven's sake, be off and take a last look at the supper-table, and see that nought is forgotten. [*Exit* PLAYFAIR *hastily.*] And you, Davy, don't 'ee stand staring like a stunpoll;—make yourself of use.

Davy. To be sure I will.

> [PRUDENCE *and* DAVY *set to work to prepare for the party.*
>
> PRUDENCE *has just placed a seat directly under the Mistletoe Bough.* DAVY, *observing this (as if without intention, and in the course of setting the room in order) removes the seat to another position, and turns away.*]

Prue. Tut, tut, tut! I declare you be more of a hindrance than a help to me any day. (*Returning.*) Only this moment I set that seat where it stood, and you must . . .

Davy (*also returning*). Tut, tut, tut! d'ye think I didn't know it, my dear. Now, see what's overhead. (*He snatches a kiss and receives back a box on the ear.*) Ay . . . !

Prue. There's to teach 'ee manners, Davy, my lad; and a proper respect for your betters.

Davy (*rubbing his cheek*). Ay . . . !—(*To himself.*) 'Tis a proper piece o' woman's flesh, and that's the truth;—but there's a sharp tongue along with it, I doubt—and a heavy hand;—*that* there is, and no mistake!

[*Knocking heard at Door* C.—*Re-enter* PLAYFAIR.]

Play. Here they are, here they are, I declare ! Come, bustle, Prudence !—the guests are at the door.

[*Enter* HOBNAIL, SWINGTREE, TUCKER, FARTHING, TIMOTHY, SOL MEIKLEJOHN, *and the other Guests.*]

Play. Walk in, ladies and gentlemen ; walk in !

Hob. Our respects to you, Steward.

Play. (*addressing various guests*).   A good-e'en to ye ; how do you do, sir?   Glad to see you, neighbour Tom Tucker :—your servant, mistress—and welcome, one and all !

Hob. A rough night, Maister.

Swing. Ay ; a rough night and a cold.

Tuck. 'Tis so.

Play. Yet we cannot complain, sonnies ;—we cannot complain.   The weather be seasonable—seasonable enow.

Tuck. So 'a be ; so 'a be.

Far. I do love to see t' ground white upon Chris'mas Day myself.

Play. Well, you be right.   For 'tis an old saying that a ' Green Yule makes a fat churchyard.'

Tuck. An old saying and a true one.

Play. So 'tis.   Ay, the weather is seasonable; and we may thank God that we ha' no cause for complaint.

A *

'Cold without and warm within' is our motto at Windy Walls at Christmas-time, neighbours . . .

Guests. Ha, ha!

Play. So, come! draw round the fire and get Jack Frost out o' your in'ards, afore the family joins us and it be time to go to supper.

[*Guests gather round the fire.*]

Sol. To supper; haw, haw!

Far. Ha, Solomon; ye 've found your tongue again, have you?

Hob. Why, the very mention o' victuals is as stirrin' to the lad's heart as the sound o' the horn was to the Owd Huntsman's in the song!

Swing. You 'll excuse his want o' manners, maister; ye know he is scarce like the rest o' us.

Davy. In short, to put it plain, the furnitur' o' his upper story is not just what ye might call *complete.*

Play. D' ye think I don't know Sol. Bless me! why I 've knowed un ever since 'a was no higher than a milking-stool. Ay; and many 's the time I 've remarked to his poor mother, when she 'd be down-in-the-mouth over her son's wool-gathering wits—'Don't 'ee be down-hearted, Susan Meiklejohn; we 'se live to see your Sol go up to Lunnon and set the Thames afire yet!' But 'a's long about it. [*Laughter.*]

Sol. (*muttering*). Haw, haw . . . It don't take much

to make some folks laugh! I should like to make some of 'em laugh on the wrong side o' their mouths.

[*Enter the* PEDLAR.]

Play. Why, it's the Pedlar! Hey, Pedlar, you are a stranger.

Ped. 'Tis as times go, master.—Anything in my line to-night?

Play. Ay; come, sit down and taste our ale; and I'll warrant you shall drive a roarin' trade among the youngsters later on.

[*The* PEDLAR, PLAYFAIR, HOBNAIL, SWINGTREE, *and* TUCKER *form a group together.*]

Ped. Ay; 'tis a twelvemonth since I was last this way, sirs.

Tuck. Lord help us! how time do fly.

Swing. It does so. Why, it seems but yesterday that we was last met round this hearth to celebrate Chris'mas.

Play. Ah! Time flies; but he brings changes with him.

Hob. A true word that, Gaffer Playfair. Ay! there was feet that danced last Christmas Eve what will not dance to-night. No, neither to-night nor yet on any Christmas Eve that is to come.

Play. True again; and nowhere truer than in the house above our heads.

Tuck. 'Tis so. Ay, Master, since this time last year, there's your son-in-law Jack Hickathrift gone. Poor Jack! a wild fellow 'a was, a swearin'-tearin' fellow; yet no man's enemy but his own.

Play. And young Willie Lee too. Now, which o' us could ha' foretold at our last merry-making that he, the Master o' the House, the flower o' the flock, the blithest and gallantest o' them all, was to be taken ere another Chris'mas Eve came round again?

Hob. Which indeed?

Ped. And yet, after all—if tales are to be believed, Master—'twas as well for him, poor chap, that ta'en he was.

Play. What do you mean?

Ped. No more than has been the talk all over the country.

Play. The talk all over the country, eh? Well don't 'ee forget, friend, that the talk all over the country will often play an unkind trick wi' dead men's names.

Ped. It may be so. I make no pretensions to know more than another man. I have been far afield. But certain 'tis that, wherever I heard the case of William Lee spoken of, 'twas whispered—not to mince matters —that, at the time of his death, there was a warrant out for his apprehension upon a charge of . . .

Guests (interrupting). Hush; for shame!

Play. I think, sir, you forget whose house you are in.

Ped. No, sir; not at all. But let me tell you that I'm a man who, when I've once spoken, will make good my words—though it be at the expense o' manners. I said that p'r'aps 'twas as well for Lee that drownded 'a was; and I maintain that, when there's a warrant . . . *o' that sort* out agen' a man, and proof behind it, that man's death by drowning is no calamity. It can only be considered *an escape !*

[*Murmurs among the Guests.*]

Play. Hush !—(*To the* PED.) You be a harsh judge, Pedlar.—Well, there's no disputing that the Master did act rashly; and the consequences of his act were grave. But that was his misfortune rather than his fault; and had it been the truth o' the story that came to your ears, I can't but believe that you'd be ready to make more allowance for Will yourself.

Tim. The truth o' the story, quotha? Now ye name that, Steward, I cannot say as how I know the *truth o' the story* myself. Not I ! though the truth o' the story ha' been told me more than once—ay, and more 'an twice or three times; still I cannot say as how I know the truth of the story yet. For why? Because 'twere told me different every time.

Hob. What's to prevent thee giving us the story now, man? You, who be, so to speak, one o' the fam'ly should know the rights o' the case, if any one.

Far. Ay; tell us all ye know, Maister; for you know more than any of us.

Play. Well, gossips! Though I 've told the story fifty times, if I 've told un once, I will e'en tell it yet once more. I would gladly do more than that for the Master's memory. A self-willed lad he was, I allow; but 'twas the worst ye could say again' him. And he was beloved by all who knew him. Ay, neighbours all! I knew him from a child myself; yet never know'd un act an unmanly part or speak an unkind word.

Davy. A born gentleman was Will.

Play. That 'a was; there are not many like him.—And now I 'll give ye the story o' his crime, and all that is known o' his end.—To begin at the beginning, you know that while Will was still in his cradle his father died and left him master of this farm. Now any one would ha' supposed that when he grew up he would ask nothing better than to live at home and enjoy it. Not at all. A ventur'some boy, bred on the coast, his heart was set on going to sea. His mother tried to win him from it; for he was her darling always; though, long before this, she had married Old Mar and had borne Cuthbert to him. But the lad would not take no for an answer; and at last he got his way. Well, the sea-faring life suited him; and he stuck to it. So time passed on, till about two years agone, when he came home on a visit. By this time his step-father had long been dead; and his mother (a widow for the second time) pressed him again to give up the sea and stay at home altogether. She pressed him sorely; yet I doubt she might ha' pressed in vain, had it not been for an orphan niece who had lately come to reside with her. But no sooner had Will set eyes on this young lady, than he was smitten with her charms; so that, when Miss Isabella came to join her persuasions to his mother's, there was no saying nay at all. Thus he consented to quit the sea, and took up his abode on the farm. All were glad . . .

Davy. All but one.

Play. Hey?

Davy. Cuthbert, the hungry Cuthbert. No man, used to play first fiddle, is best pleased to step down and take second place.

Tuck. 'Taint in natur'!

Play. Be that as it may, it is no business of ours. The farm had belonged to Will's father, not to Cuthbert's; and Cuthbert had not even a younger brother's interest in it. He had no more title to it than you or I.—But to proceed. The young Master had not been long at home before we were told that he had got his heart's desire, and was betrothed to his Cousin Bell. The times were good for farmers; for the war kept prices high; and everything seemed to be prospering to a wish.—But it's an old saying that 'tis a wise man who knows when 'a 's well off;—and that's what Will

never knew. He had houses, land, and money; his
mother worshipped him; he was liked by all who knew
him, and betrothed to the girl of his choice:—you
might think that he would be content to spend the rest
of his days in peace and quiet? Not he.—As time
went on, we began to notice that he frequently left
home, and would sometimes remain absent for a day or
two at a time. What was more, when he returned he told
us little or nothing as to where he'd been, and would
turn off all questions with a joke. My daughter and I
were among the first to notice this; because, whenever
Will went from home, my daughter's husband—who had
also been a sailor—went from home as well. (Will had
before this singled out my son-in-law to be his chosen
follower; so 'twas plain that wherever Will now went
Jack went along with him.) Well, when Jack had been
absent once or twice, my daughter—as was natural
enough—would give him no peace till he should tell
her where he had been.

Prue. Not likely.

Play. At first he tried to put her off with cock-and-
bull stories;—but 'twas no good. When a woman
makes up her mind to discover a secret, trust her to
gain her end—particularly if the secret be her husband's!
At last the truth came out.

Ped. What was it?

Play. You shall hear. Like every one else in these

parts, Will had seen more or less of the carrying on of the contraband trade. As we all know, the profits are large if the smugglers have luck in outwitting the Revenue men. Now, Will didn't want money, but he wanted excitement:—maybe too, he had still a hankering after the old sea life. Anyhow, some evil genius put the notion in his head to try his fortune as a free-trader. He did not stay to think twice ;—but procures a boat, gets together a crew o' lawless characters (with Jack among 'em) fro' the neighbourhood, and there he stands —as accomplished a leader of smugglers as any on our coast !—And this, as Jack confessed, was the secret of his mysterious absences.

Ped. H'm ! Playing with edged tools, eh ?

Play. Well, at first all went smoothly enough. Will was an artful fellow when 'a pleased ;—and for a time he contrived to ply his trade without awakening the suspicions of the Coastguard. But at last the day of reckoning came ;—and this is how it happened. On the 25th day of January last, if your business had chanced to take you down to the sea-banks, near the spot they call the Green Haven, towards nightfall, you might ha' spied, where she lay-to in the offing, a smart little cutter. This smart little cutter was Will's boat, the *Blue-eyed Maid ;* and she 'd a cargo of strong waters aboard, which the smugglers intended, if fortune favoured 'em, to land in the haven that night. They had taken their usual precautions by exchanging signals with a friend on shore (whom, in their own slang, they called their spotsman) and had learnt that there was nought to be feared that night from the Coastguard, who were gone off to attend to a job in another direction.   Darkness closed in.   The moon rose late that night; and the smugglers now only waited till the tide should suit to land their tubs.   Meantime, they sat in their cabin, and passed the time drinking and playing cards.   All at once—without note o' warning —their watch on deck gives the alarm for the Revenue men.   Impossible!—but no, 'twas true enough.   The Coastguard's departure had been a feint to throw dust in the eyes of the spotsman ; and there, sure enough, they now were, rowing silently out to pay a midnight visit on board the *Blue-eyed Maid ;*—and so dark was the night and so noiseless had been their advance, that they were within pistol-shot ere the Smugglers got wind of their approach.   Instantly the alarm was given, and all hands rushed on deck.   The captain of the Coast- guard saw it, and shouted to his boat's crew to give way. For the smugglers, 'twas a choice 'twixt fight or flight— and precious little time to think about it.   To avoid bloodshed, Will, their leader, chose to fly ; and gave the word to put the vessel's head before the wind and run for the open sea.—But the time was too short.   Before the smugglers could get their sails trimmed, the bows of the Revenue cutter had overlapped their stern . . .

Ped. God bless us !

Play. The captain of the King's men—a mortal foe to smugglers—shouts to his men, and cutlass in hand, leaps aboard the *Blue-eyed Maid.*—Will saw it. He wore a pistol in his belt ; and in the heat o' the moment he draws it, takes aim—and fires.—The captain fell—fell back into his own boat—and fell to rise no more.

Guests. Ah !

Play. When they saw their capt'n fall, the Preventive men lost heart, and held back for a minute or two. This gave Will's crew time to get off ;—but ere they had gone far, they saw that their enemies had recovered 'emselves and were bent on giving chase.—The two cutters were evenly matched ; there was a fresh breeze blowing, and an exciting race began. Away they went. The deck of the *Blue-eyed Maid* was a scene of confusion—each man labouring to his utmost to press the boat forward.—All at once there was a cry of ' *Man overboard ; 'bout ship ; down with the helm !* ' The cry was from Jack ; and the man overboard was Will. Now Will could swim ; but as ill-luck would have it, he wore sea-boots :—they filled, and he sank. Jack saw this : he would have followed his master to the end of the world, and, crying once more to the crew to put the boat about, he now plunged after him over the side.—But the crew had lost their heads :—to them to put about meant capture ; so they held on their course—leaving Will and Jack to their fate,—and, to cut the story short, in the end got clear away.

Ped. And the men overboard?

Play. The smugglers had reckoned, no doubt, that Will and Jack would be picked up by the Revenue cutter, which was close astern ;—and preferred that two of their number should fall into the clutches of the law rather than that all should do so. But the Coastguard must have passed the two men by in the darkness without observing them ; and the long and short of the matter is that neither the one nor the other has been seen or heard of since.—And now you know as much as I do myself of the story of William Lee.

Ped. The men's bodies were never recovered, as I understand?

Play. They were not. And this at first inclined us to hope that they might perhaps, by some means or other, have escaped a watery grave. It was by some held likely that they might be lurking in concealment till the search which was made for 'em should cool, and the noise of their doings be quieted down.—For they had been recognised; and there was a warrant out against Will, on the charge of having caused the officer's death, with a reward of fifty guineas offered by Gover'ment for his apprehension. However, their escape after all could only ha' been by a miracle; —and when weeks and months passed and they gave no sign, the most hopeful of us were fain at last to abandon hope.

Davy. Ay, ay. They're food for fishes long ere this, poor souls !

Ped. I don't feel sure of that. With a price set upon his capture, Lee would naturally be shy of showing himself. It' may be that he and his comrade are only giving the law the slip all the time.

Tuck. Of course it may. Never despair, say I :—who knows but some fine day will bring both of 'em home again yet ?

Far. I should not be surprised.

Play. No, neighbours, no ;—you are leaving the circumstances o' the case out of your count. In the first place, Will and Jack were not the fellows to be easily scared. Then, remember that the young Master was on the eve of marriage ;—and at such a time 'twill take more than the terrors o' the law to keep a man away from his sweetheart. Then again, there is the Mistress. Will could not fail to understand what a sad affliction—as God knows the reality has proved—the mere report of his death must be to his poor mother ;— and if he had been alive—though he could not come himself—he would assuredly have sent her a token.

Tuck. Suppose 'twere not in his power to send a token either ?

Play. You suppose too much.

Swing. I remember once hearing a story of a token sent from beyond the grave.

Davy. That must ha' been a queer story, son!

Swing. The man who told it declared it was true.

[*Three knocks are heard at the door.*]

Play. Why, who can this be? We're all present.

Davy. They do say that three raps on the door, by an unseen hand, means *death.*

Prue. Be quiet! why will you talk like that? Mark my words, you will live to repent it!

Play. Whoever it may be, we must not keep un standing outside.—(*In a louder voice.*) Come in!

[*Enter* OLD HICKATHRIFT.]

Old H. A good e'en to ye all!

Play. 'Pon my life, it's Daddy Hickathrift!

Davy. Hey, daddy;—what, still to the fore?

Play. We scarcely expected to see you to-night.

Old H. I ha' risen from my bed and put on my clo'es a' purpose to join 'ee, souls.

Play. Well done!

Old H. 'Tis the first time these many months.

Play. Well done again! Come; you be the oldest here; the place of honour in the elbow-chair is yours. Sit ye down. We were just speaking of your son—poor fellow.

Old H. Eh?

Play. We were speaking of Jack.

Old H. Ay, lack-a-day;—poor Jack! 'a was a good son.

Tuck. So 'a was.—But you must keep your spirits up ;—I was saying only just now that maybe you'll see un back again yet!

Old H. I cannot hear 'ee.

Tuck. Maybe you'll see him back again yet!

Old H. Why, so I shall.

Tuck. D' ye think so now?

Old H. I'm sure of it.

Tuck. That's right.—(*Aside to the other Guests*). It's plain to me, neighbours, that the owd gen'l'man's mind is failing him ;—why 'tis only a minute agone that 'a spoke of his son as a dead man.

Old H. I shall not ha' long to wait either.

Tuck. Why ;—what d'ye mean ?

Old H. I mean this—that I expect, please God, to see my son Jack to-night.

Tuck. To-night !—Lord help us !

Davy. There are the queerest notions i' the old boy's head—'tis a perfect curiosity-shop for 'em ! Listen, all of ye :—I'll ply him with questions, and I'll warrant you shall hear summat that will surprise ye.

Far. Go ahead !

Davy (*to Old H.*). Come, gaffer ;—what makes 'ee think that you will see your son to-night? Tell us that.

Old H. Well,—I'll tell 'ee.

Davy. Do so.—(*To the Guests.*) Now, hark!

Old H. It is Christmas Eve.

Davy. So it is;—but what o' that?

Old H. Christmas Eve . . . 'tis the night when the Saviour of mankind was born on earth—the holiest night in all the year.

Davy. So 'tis, so 'tis;—but what o' that?

Old H. To-night the cock crows all night long.

Davy. Why, so folk say. [*He winks at the Guests.*]

Old H. And the bees i' the hives sing a hymn of praise.

Davy. Ay;—so they do. [*He winks again.*]

Old H. And the cattle i' the stalls fall down on their knees to worship.

Davy (*to the Guests*). D'ye hear that?—(*To Old H.*) Well, what besides?

Old H. And to-night, the Powers of Darkness . . .

Davy. The Powers o' Darkness, hey, daddy?

Old H. The Powers o' Darkness lose their sway. And the dead . . .

Davy. The dead . . . ?

Old H. Ay, the dead put on their earthly shapes . . . and return to their homes . . .

Davy. And return to their homes . . . !

Old H. To dine and dance with the living.

Davy. To dine and dance wi' the living!

All. God bless us!

Old H. But, at cock-crow, when the morning breaks, they return to whence they came. [*A pause.*]

Davy (*breaking the silence*). Ha, ha, ha!—Did ye ever hear the like o' that, sonnies?

Play. Nay, lad;—there be nought to laugh at there. 'Tis an ancient superstition.

Ped. A strange one, in faith!

Tuck. But no one believes in en nowadays.

Play. Our forefathers believed in it, nevertheless;—and in many no less strange.

Swing. They knew no better.

Davy. How they must ha' shook in their shoes o' Christmas time!

Play (*shaking his head*). The strangest beliefs are not always the least true.

Tuck. But no one believes the like nowadays.

Play. Except it be the old man there;—and he, poor body, is no longer what 'a once was. In his mind (as will sometimes happen wi' men o' his years) the old stories that 'a heard in childhood have outlasted weightier matters.

Swing. Is he failing?

Play. I see a greater difference in him within the last twelve months than in as many years before. But he's not alone in that. If you have not seen the mistress since she lost her son, you will see a great change in her too.

Swing. Do you say so?

Play. That I do. For ye remember the active, managing lady she was—always the first to rise in the morning and the last to lie down at night;—and so clever at her business that it used to be said on the place that she could teach every man of us his work?— as fine and strapping a figure of a woman, too, as you shall see on a summer's day;—though inclined to silence always and reserved. She's an altered creature now! When the news of Will's drowning first reached her, 'twould ha' made your heart bleed to see. Not a tear did she shed—not one, you may believe me;—but just bowed her head, and cried aloud that her grey hairs were brought wi' sorrow to the grave! So, from the very first, she put no trust in the hopes held out that her son might be alive. And since that day Care has not left her for a moment. No art avails to cheer her. But she will sit for hours together with eyes fixed on the ground, the very pictur' o' Grief;—or, if she goes about her daily tasks, 'tis with never a word or a smile, but silent and mournful—like a Phantom from another world.—There's no measuring the depth of a mother's love, neighbours.

Hob. Ah, that's God's truth!

Ped. Does Cuthbert fill his brother's place in the house now?

Davy. Ay;—more than that, I shall not be surprised to see un fill it in another quarter too.

Tuck. With his cousin . . . ?

Davy. That's the size of it !

Play. Hush ! I hear them.

[*Enter* CUTHBERT, MRS. MAR, *and* ISABELLA.]

Cuth. Good evening, good folks ;—and welcome, each and all ! I'm glad to see ye.

Hob. Our service to ye, sir.

Swing. And to the mistress.

Tuck. And the young lady.

Cuth. My thanks to you, gentlemen.—And now, listen to me. We are met here to-night to enjoy ourselves—to enjoy ourselves, d'ye hear me ?—Playfair !

Play. Sir ?

Cuth. Have my orders been attended to ?

Play. They have, sir.

Cuth. My orders were that neither food nor firing should be spared, that all may spend a happy evening.

Guests. Hear, hear !

Cuth. As for the drink, eh, Timothy Chilblain ? we'll trust that to take care o' itself?

Tim. I thank'ee, maister :—to my mind 'enough's as good as a feast' any day ;—more by token, there's a day when enough is better than a feast—and that day's the day after.

Guests. Haw, haw, haw !

Cuth. Pshaw !—Still, if proverbs be your only stock-

in-trade, my fine fellow, I have plenty worth two o'
that;—'A hair o' the dog that bit ye;'—'What kills
cures' . . . The day after! why, to-morrow's Christmas! The old song says—

> *' What they could not eat that night,*
> *They ate next morning fried'* . . .

Guests. Ha, ha, ha!

Cuth. We'll do the same!

Tuck. Ha, ha, ha!—'tis a merry gentleman.

Far. And a free-spoken.

Swing. And an open-handed as ever was!

Davy. Long life to him!

Guests. So say we all.   [CUTHBERT *bows.*]

Cuth. But what, in the name of everything that's
gloomy, was keeping ye all so quiet just now? I protest
I should never have guessed that you were in the house!

Play. We were talking of your brother, sir.

Cuth. Ha!—of William. Alas! poor fellow;—cut
off in the flower of his age, full of life and spirits. A
sad fate his.

Guests. Poor fellow!

Cuth. And a finer fellow never stept:—daring, yet
gentle;—open-hearted;—honest as the day!

Swing. 'A was all that.

Hob. And more besides.

Cuth. 'Twill be long before we see his like again!—Yet,
though none knew his value better than I, good folks—

still, I am one who holds that, even in our mourning for departed friends, there is a certain *discretion* to be observed.—Am I right, goodman Tucker?

Tuck. Sure-ly!

Cuth. Surely.—I would not, you understand, forget that sooner or later all of us must die . . .

Swing. So us must!

Cuth. That brothers, sons, friends, kindred, are dying every day;—that all must at some time or other experience the regret which we now feel;—that it is useless —and worse than useless—to indulge an ineffectual grief;—and, in fine, that we 've a duty to the living as well as to the dead.

Tuck. That's true.

Cuth. Which duty requires us to cheer up;—not to give way;—to do what we can to cheer one another . . . And that is why I have given this party to-night!— At my request, my fair cousin has at last consented to lay aside the black frock she wore for Will;—and I hope, ere long, to see my mother follow suit; eh, mother . . . ?—What, have you not a word to say to the neighbours and work-folk? 'Tis but a cold welcome they get from you to-night!

Mrs. M. I *have* a word to say to them.—Friends, this is not the first time we meet, and I think you are most of ye acquainted with my dealings as a neighbour . . .

Hob Ay; that we be, mistress.

Mrs. M. And deeds, after all, are still worth more than words.—You have heard Cuthbert:—others have said the same. They mean well, I dare say;—but I know their arguments by heart, and am sick to death of hearing them. They tell me that sons die every day . . . I grant they do:—that scores of mothers have suffered as I suffer . . . What's that to me? So much the worse for them, that's all I know; so much the worse for them! It does not profit me.—And they speak of the healing power of Time;—they say Time brings consolation:—but I tell you that to a grief like mine Time can bring no consolation. How should it? Will Time bring back what I have lost; he in whom my hopes were centred,—my son, the delight of his mother's eyes, the joy of her heart, the comfort of her declining years? Will Time bring him back? Not so!—And shall Time teach me to forget him? No:— forgetting is for those who would forget! Enough.— Had I been mistress in this house, there should have been no feasting here to-night. But I'm no longer mistress, as it seems.—The table's laid. I wish you hearty appetite! [*She drops a curtsey and goes out.*]

Cuth. Poor mother! Her affliction is in truth a heavy one. But you must not notice her hard words:—she doesn't mean what she says.—(*To himself.*) How much cast down they look! To think that there be mules in the world who won't even enjoy themselves when that's

what you ask of 'em . . . ! to-night too, when I'd
promised myself my fill of the sweets of Power and
Popularity!—No matter. Let me but pour the liquor
down their throats :—'tis a specific never known to fail.
—(*Aloud.*) And now, good folks, the feast awaits us
spread in the next room! When we have ate and
drunk till we can eat and drink no more—and not before—we'll come back here and have some music. I
am fond of music . . . music, which, as poets feign, was
born in heaven. It shall transport our spirits thither-
ward to-night. For it shall pour sweet inspiration into
tender hearts, until they fill and overflow :—in madcap
brains that laugh at love, it shall put frolic, folly, licence,
and a thousand mischievous devices :—and it shall take
the oldest, most decrepit pair o' legs among us—'pon my
soul it shall!—and set 'em once more a-jigging and
frisking in the gayest measures of their prime!—Come;
—you should be ready for your suppers. Follow me;
—I'll show the way!

> [*He gives his hand to* ISABELLA *and leads her to the
> Supper-room. The rest follow.*]

Far. (*to Tim. as they pass out*). There's no arguin' of
likes and mislikes. I never liked that Cuthbert. And,
though his treatment of us to-night is handsomeness
itself, as I'm a living sinner, I dunnot like en yet!

Tim. The ungrateful soul of you!

> [*Exeunt omnes. A long pause.*]

[*Enter C.* WILLIAM LEE *and* JACK.]

Will. At home once more !

Jack. Sure enough.

Will. Thank God ; thank God !

Jack. We may do that.—Ay, Master Will ; it 's a strange thing to be at home again when a man 's been long away !

Will. I never felt the strangeness of it before as I do to-night.—(*Thoughtfully.*) It is strange indeed ; and sweet . . . yet there 's sadness in it too. For as I look once more on this old room, on the time-worn household furniture—the selfsame which I remember long ago—the tears, I scarce know why, spring to my eyes.

Jack. 'Tis a mortal strange thing to come home again when a man 's been long away.

Will. 'Tis a moment I shall not forget. A blessing on the name of home, Jack ; a blessing on it ! there 's no music speaks so sweetly to the wanderer's ear as that word—none so touchingly. To the sailor home is a fair haven in the midst of stormy seas.—And a blessing upon this old house—the home of my childhood, the dwelling-place of all I hold dear on earth—a blessing on it ! Time, that brings so many changes, has left this at least unchanged.

Jack. Why, so 'a have. Plague on it now, if everything

b'aint exac'ly as we left un—down to the very horse-shoes hung up above chimbley for luck !—By this hand ! to look round you, skipper, ye might a'most take an oath that we'd never been away.   It might all ha' been a dream ;—it might all ha' been a dream fro' beginnin' to end !

Will. I'm surprised that there's no one about, Jack. Where can they be ?

[*Convivial sounds are heard proceeding from the Supper-room.*]

. . . What's that ?

Jack. It sounds uncommon like as though the folks was keepin' Christmas.

Will. In the master's absence ?   I don't think so.

Jack. We shall soon see. (*Goes up stage to door* L, *left open.*)   Keeping Chris'mas they be, Master Will . . . and keepin' it in what's called the *good old style*, too ! (WILL. *goes up stage.*)   See for yourself.—Won't they open their eyes when we join 'em, that's all ?

Will. Stay, Jack.—I've a fancy to watch them for a bit before we show ourselves.

Jack. As you please, sir.

Will. They are noisy.—They don't seem to miss us much.

Jack. Not they !

Will. (standing by the doorway which commands a view of the Supper-room). Not they.—See! the board creaks beneath its load . . . and now the toast goes round. Cuthbert is host; he plays the part to perfection : and Isabel is by his side, all smiles. The yokels swill and gorge to heart's content, and for the hour forget that they are mortal. My mother alone is absent . . . *(Turning away.)* No; they don't seem to miss us much !

Jack (by the doorway). Cheerly now, skipper . . . hist, I say! There's one o' the company has risen from table and comes this way.

Will. Who is it ?

Jack. Why, who should it be ? Who but the girl o' your choice, your fancy lass, your sweetheart . . .

Will. Isabella !—*(To himself.)* She, at least, has no heart for these rejoicings . . . yet she looked gay enough just now. I've been long away; and they say that absence alters the fondest hearts . . . Is she unchanged ?

Jack (overhearing the last words). If she be changed at all, 'tis that she looks fresher and bonnier than before.—By my troth! she's as blooming as the month of May, and blushes like the rose.

Will. I'd as lief she had been paler; for faithful love should surely have looked pale.—*(To himself.)* Oh, it is base in me to doubt her even for a moment . . . Yet *(observing the screen)* how easily I might satisfy my doubts.

(*He hesitates.*) They shall be satisfied! If I wrong her, be it hers to shame me by her truth.—(*Aloud; pointing to the screen.*) In, Jack; under cover, and lie close.

Jack. What's in the wind now?

Will. I mean to see. [*Draws him behind the screen.*]

[*Enter* ISABELLA.]

Isa. I've contrived to slip away! The heat and noise were overpowering; and the country-folk are good for another couple of hours at least before they rise. Cuthbert could not in reason expect my patience to hold out. It was only fortunate that all were too busy to notice my escape! (*Seats herself.*) And now, how shall I pass the time? At my embroidery-frame . . . No, I am tired of that. Or shall I read a page? No, nor that either. I'm in an idle mood to-night; 'tis Christmas Eve, and it shall be a holiday. Besides, I want to think. I have much to think over—such things, too, as I cannot think over except when I'm alone . . . Well! 'tis quiet enough in here.—I confess I like to get the place to myself at times . . . at this moment, at least, it is pleasant—after the noisy assemblage I have just left close at hand.—Yet, truth to tell, it is not very often I should care to be by myself after twilight in this house; for there are times when I could easily believe that it is haunted. I'm sure it's old and lonely and dull enough to harbour ghosts in legions. And I 've heard strange noises too . . . but they tell me it 's only the wind. Only the wind? The wind plays strange tricks here, then, that 's all I know. It lifts the carpets, and takes hold of the doors in passing and rattles them, as though 'twould force an entrance. And then it will tap slily on the window-pane in the night-time; or moan for hours together in the chimney, with a voice like Old Age lamenting over happy days, gone never to return. Heigh-ho! Only the wind . . . well! the house was well named Windy Walls.

[*Enter* CUTHBERT *behind.*]

[*He closes the Supper-room door and advances unseen by* ISABELLA.]

Cuth. A penny for your thoughts, cousin !

Isa. Cuthbert ! how you startled me.

Cuth. Were you thinking of me, then ? (*Bows.*) I am honoured;—for, as you well know, 'tis more to me to be in your thoughts than in any other's favour.

Isa. A pretty speech to please a lady's ear—hey, cousin ? But how come you to have left the supper-table ?

Cuth. Bluntly, and without circumlocution,—I left it because you did.

Isa. Then, no less bluntly, and without circumlocution, you have done foolishly. To your place, sir !

Cuth. To my place? Where, if not here, is my place?

Isa. At the head of the supper-table.

Cuth. Then yours is by my side.

Isa. I don't admit it.

Cuth. Then I, in turn, take leave to dispute your judgment, shift my position, and assert that my place is by *your* side.

[*Seats himself.*]

Isa. Nay, Cuthbert;—do not ask me to go back. 'Tis a penance I protest against.

Cuth. Very well;—I will not ask you to go back.— I'll stay beside you here instead.

Isa. Indeed you must not.

Cuth. Pray, why?—Do you prefer my room to my company?

Isa. There's no need for me to say so. But what will your guests say?—Remember, you are Master here now.

Cuth. True enough.

Isa. Then, as such, you have your duties:—let me see you return to them.

Cuth. One moment, and your harsh command shall be obeyed.—Yes, Isabella, what you say is true enough. I am Master here now;—I may claim that the farm is mine, or as good as mine.—My poor brother was the last of his race;—on his death, his estate reverted to his mother—that is, to my mother. It is hers to do with as she pleases;—and, naturally enough, she will please that, on her death, it shall descend to me—her only surviving son.—Now, without vainglory, this farm is a fair property. 'Tis true the land is somewhat poor;—but there's enough of it. It is well-stocked, too—excellent well. Then I find that my predecessors (like sensible men) have been content to live within their income. There's money to the name of Mar in the County Bank, cousin,—a sum not to be despised.

Isa. (*with indifference*). Indeed !

Cuth. A sum not to be despised !—Again, my position in the world is better than what ye might think. True, I am but a farmer—a tiller of the soil ;—yet I don't need to fear to hold my head up spite o' that. For, believe me, there be plenty who dub 'emselves gentlemen that would jump to change purses—or for that matter pedigrees either—with the plain farmer of Windy Walls !

Isa. I don't dispute it. No doubt there are hundreds who envy you.

Cuth. That well may be. For let me tell you, Miss Isabella, that I can boast that which whosoever boasts shall see mankind bow down before him.

Isa. Ah ;—and what may that be ?

Cuth. That I'm a rich man !—yes ; I am now beyond the reach of hunger, beyond the reach of misery, sorrow, and distress :—for me the ills of life have lost their

terrors.—I need care for no man. I can afford to
laugh at my enemies—and I am one who has always
had enemies :—I can afford to laugh at my friends—and
I shall now have many friends. I can afford to snap
my fingers at the world !—I am a free man—in this free
country, 'tis the rich alone are free—and every free man
is a king;—king of the only kingdom worth the ruling
—king of his own life—of his years, of his talents, of
his destiny !

Isa. You ought to be content if any man is. But,
with what object you tell all this to me, I own myself at
a loss to conceive.

Cuth. You will soon know.—Isabella, I am *not*
content.

Isa. Have you not all that heart could wish?

Cuth. Not I !

Isa. Then you must be hard to satisfy.

Cuth. Perhaps I am.—Hear me, cousin. When you
sat by my side at supper just now, I looked first at
you, and then at all the beauties of the neighbourhood
seated round about. There were some fair faces among
them—fit to be your handmaids;—but you were the
queen of them all !

Isa. Cuthbert !

Cuth. And when you rose, and tript so daintily to the
door and left the room, the feast—so far as 'twas a feast
for me—was at an end.—I could not stay behind. I

also rose and followed you.—And when I found you here, alone, I felt that at last my star was in the ascendant;—that this was a lucky hour brought about by my good genius, and perhaps not to recur . . .

Isa. (*faintly*). I don't understand . . .

Cuth. Then I'll speak plainer. I felt that the moment was come for me to lay my worldly possessions at your feet, cousin; to bid you be mistress of Windy Walls; to ask you to be my wife.—I love you, Isabel!

Isa. (*struggling with her agitation*). You take my breath away!

Cuth. Your answer?

Isa. My answer . . . O Cuthbert! indeed it is too soon to talk like that.

Cuth. Too soon!—how so?

Isa. You cannot have forgotten . . .

Cuth. Forgotten?

Isa. Yes, forgotten—since you force me to speak out —how my troth was plighted to your brother.

Cuth. No; I have not forgotten that.—But what of it, cousin—seeing that poor William is no more?

Isa. (*sadly*). Poor William is no more . . . Who knows that?

Cuth. Every one.

Isa. You are wrong;—no one knows it.

Cuth. Pshaw! there's not a doubt of it.

Isa. There is no proof.—If he were to return?

Cuth. He will not return.

Isa. Dead men have returned ere now.

Cuth. I say he will *not* return.

Isa. Who can tell?

Cuth. I say he will not return: I say he will never return—*till the sea gives up her dead !*

Isa. Hush, hush ! For Heaven's sake, don't talk like that, Cuthbert ;—you fill me with uneasiness.—Just hark how the wind is howling.

Cuth. Ay ; 'tis a wild night (*he goes to the window and opens the shutter*), and dark, though the ground is white with snow.—See ! how the snow-flakes whirl—distracted beings, urged madly hither and thither by the blasts of overmastering Necessity. 'Tis on such nights as this, Isabel, that flocks are lost upon the hills ; shepherds perish in the snow ; and homeless wayfarers sink to rest in ditches, to be found there, stiff and frozen, on the morrow.—An insidious enemy the Snow ! for he will not spring openly at his victim's throat, but will sap the strength of his limbs with a grateful weariness, dull the keenness of his brain with a flattering heaviness, and take the voice of a friend to whisper, 'Sleep !'—when to sleep is death. (*Turning from the window.*) It blows from the nor'-east. Sea-farers will have cause to curse this night, my pretty cousin ; for many's the good ship will drive on our ironbound coast with the gale.

Isa. God have mercy on the sailors !

c *

Cuth. Let Him have mercy on them, an He will!
Yet there be landsmen not a few, let me tell ye, who
will not reproach Him should His mercy fail.—For to-
morrow,—when the clouds break away and the winds
are still once more, when the sun shines out, and the
billows, small and infantine, break gently and peacefully
upon the shore—as if they knew no other mood,—to-
morrow, the beach should be strewn with a glorious
harvest for the coastsmen :—good wreck-timber, enough
to keep a man in roaring fires as long as winter lasts;
casks full o' spirits; boxes full o' clothes; and stores of
every kind.—Why, there ain't an old witch in the parish,
whose rickety stumps will carry her so far, but to-morrow
she'll be making for the shore as if life depended on it,
to pick up and carry off whatever luck may cast in her
way !—So, one man's poison is another's meat, you see.

Isa. They profit by the ruin of others ;—but their
hearts must smite them for it.

Cuth. Not at all !—What would you have ?   Folks
must live, you know ;—and, bless you, the owners have
no further need for their property.   Not they ! for there,
face downward, in the sand they lie : cold men, whom
now no blazing logs—though ye piled 'em to the sky—
should warm again : sober men, in whose hearts no
liquor—were it ne'er so fiery—shall ever rouse the old
wanton humour more !—And such a man, my gentle
cousin, is your old sweetheart, Will.

Isa. (*shedding tears*). Alas ! poor Will !

Cuth. Poor Will, poor Will !—But enough of such sombre speculation . . . This is Christmas Eve (though we seem to have forgotten it), the season when all who care not for wind or weather make merry and rejoice.— Shall we be merry, coz?—how say you? See ! above our heads there hangs a branch of mistletoe ;—'tis the symbol of youthful pleasures, the delight of fond lovers at Christmas-tide.—Before the night is one hour older, a hundred pairs of loving lips will have met beneath its shade. But, just now, the room is empty . . . we are alone. Dearest, most beautiful and best, you will not let me speak as I would speak . . .

Isa. No, no.

Cuth. Yet grant me this—that our lips be the first to meet beneath that bough.

Isa. No, no.

Cuth. You would not refuse me such a little thing? Come ; a wilful man must have his way. [ISA. *is silent.*] —My own . . . cousin !

[*She allows him to take her hand and lead her under the mistletoe :—he has his back to the screen ; she has her face to it. As he is in the act of pressing his lips to hers,* WILLIAM *suddenly comes out from his concealment with a gesture forbidding the kiss.*]

[ISABELLA *shrieks.*]

Cuth. Isabella?

Isa. (*pointing*). Cuthbert! Cuthbert! I see a drowned man, with drenched hair and glassy eyes, and clothes all dripping wet!

Cuth. Great Heaven!

Will. I forbid you in God's name.

Isa. (*hiding her face*). 'Tis the wraith of my dead sweetheart come back to reproach me with my falsehood.

Cuth. No, no ;—'tis Will himself!

Will. She was mine before she was yours!

Cuth. Ay. But, brother, before Heaven, we believed that your claim had been set aside by a Power which, in this world, is supreme, and brooks no contradiction. We believed your claim had been set aside by the hand of Death itself.

Will. So it seems ; so it seems indeed!

Jack. Yet here we be. Here's the master safe and sound ;—and here am I, Jack Hickathrift, come back— like a bad penny-piece, as the sayin' is.

Cuth. I can scarce believe my senses.

Will. And I would to Heaven I could doubt mine!— Often and often I have heard it said that there's not a man among us, from the humble bread-winner among the poor to the skeely pilot seated at the helm o' the State—that there is not a man among us, so grandly gifted, so sublime of soul, or alas! so well-beloved—but, let him be taken away . . . another will arise to fill his place ; and the sun will shine and the winds blow, the showers will fall and the flowers bloom ; maidens marry and men go a-marketing, just as before ;—and the wide_ world jog on, not an inch i' the hour the slower for the loss of him !

Jack. I trow 'tis no more than the truth, skipper !

Will. Yet I never felt the truth of it till now ! And a hard truth it is to lie under a sick man's pillow when he feels his end draw nigh.—O Cuthbert, O Isabella ! but a moment ago I spoke of this house as unchanged ; —how shall I now speak of the dwellers in the house ? Among them Change has not been so idle . . . Forsooth ! if we contrast the lasting nature of man's handiwork with the fickleness of man himself, the pride of life is quickly humbled. For what we fashion with our hands will last its day ; but what we feel in our hearts ! we cannot keep that from decay—nor would not though we could.—Will you break the news of my return to our mother, brother ?

Cuth. Gladly ;—and you may trust me to be gentle, for I know her high-wrought nature.

Will. That is well.

Jack (to CUTH.*).* Then I 'll e'en go along wi' you, sir.

[*Exit* CUTHBERT.]

Jack (to himself). My Prudence will expect to get a kiss of me first, I s'pose ; and my owd father a shake o'

the hand : and then, belike, at last I shall get a drop
o' summat to wet my whistle ;—and, by. my soul, my
throat 's like a furnace !   [*Exit* JACK.]

Will. We are alone.—O Isabel ! O Isabel ! and it is
thus we meet !

Isa. William . . .

Will. (*wildly*). Your vows, your pledges, your pro-
testations, where are they ? . . . As well ask of the
flowers of last spring, where are they ? But stay . . .
Come nearer the light, girl ; let me look at you. Surely
you are not the same I wooed and won.—My sweetheart
loved me well ; she swore a thousand times that she 'd
be true to me. This cannot be she. Come to the light,
come away ; let me look at you. [*He takes her head
between his hands and gazes in her face.*]

Isa. William !

Will. Hush ! . . . It is a marvellous resemblance
. . . no, 'tis the same face.—Yes ; these eyes are the
same dear eyes,—whilom my stars that ruled my
destiny ; these fair lips are the lips that I have kissed,
likening 'em to roses—a foolish figure lovers use ; and
this white brow—the chosen home of Candour, as
I thought it—is the brow of her I loved. It is the
same.

Isa. O William, spare me ! Your reproaches may
have been deserved, but spare me this. [*She breaks
from him.*]

Will. (beside himself). But no, no, no ! It is not the same ; it is not the same. The eyes are the same, the lips are the same, and the brow the same . . . but the heart is changed. That kiss ! 'twas the passing bell of a dead love ; and my old love is no more ! She and I will meet no more !

Isa. William ! this is madness, or most like it. Spare yourself, spare me this misery.

Will. No more, no more !

Isa. Hear me ; I may have been to blame ; but you are unjust to me, indeed you are. Living, I never wronged you ; and, before Heaven, I believed you dead to-night !

Will. No more !

Isa. I was not alone. Your mother, all in this house believed you dead, and mourned for you ; and you suffered us to mourn. But I will not upbraid you with your cruelty ; neither, in my heart, can I tax myself with failing in my duty. You are unjust to me, indeed you are.

Will. Perhaps I am ;—it was ever my besetting sin that I was of too quick and jealous a temper. Will you forgive me ?

Isa. With my whole heart—as I would ask for your forgiveness.

Will. It is yours. Come, dry your eyes ; sit by my side, and let us talk as we were used to.

Isa. Of what shall we talk ?

Will. Of what you will . . . only not of old times—
for old times are forgotten; nor of lovers' vows—for
lovers' vows are nought.—But there, enough; I'll choose
the theme—one that shall match my mood.

Isa. As you please, cousin.

Will. Then we'll talk of death.

Isa. Of death!

Will. Ay; and of the dead.

Isa. But what will you find to say on such a sombre
theme?

Will. Oh, enough; enough in all conscience.   There
lies no lack of matter there for the dullest and most
barren of preachers.—Fair cousin, you believed me
dead . . .

Isa. I did, indeed.

Will. And you grieved for me?

Isa. Bitterly, and from my soul.

Will. I believe you, and commend your tender heart.
—Yet learn this lesson of me, child;—that though you had
grieved for me ten, ay twenty, times as bitterly, you had
yet not grieved enough.—Sweet girl; dear Isabel! you
are young: as yet you have known but the bright side
of life; what wonder if you have given few thoughts to
what is most cruel, most inexorable?   But Time and
Sorrow bring Knowledge to us all.   Ere you quit my
side to-night, you shall be a sadder and a wiser woman.
—You believed me dead.   Did you ever consider the

dead man's lot? Perhaps not:—consider it now.—
Methinks it is a hard lot. He is one who has known
better days: for he has known the thing called Life:—
to stand erect upon a green and beauteous earth; warmed
by the kindly beams of a glorious sun; rejoicing in its
light. He has tasted of the pride of strength, which
says 'I will do this,' 'do that' . . . and straightway it is
done. He has known affection; the warm-hearted
fellowship of friends; he has known love. O Isabel!
though he was the humblest of mortals, I tell you that his
lot was then a king's lot!—And it is changed; for him,
old times are no more: but, far off from the voices and
the smiles of friends, he sits, with idle hands—alone,
forlorn—amid the everlasting twilight, and looks back
upon golden opportunities foregone, while the days and
the hours were yet his.

Isa. How strangely you talk, Will!

Will. Strangely, sweet?

Isa. Yes, strangely; for I never heard death spoken
of as you speak of it before. Perhaps you have been
very near it;—but, to hear you, one might take you to
be some adventurous traveller—the first to penetrate that
Unknown Country—who now brings back his report.

Will. And that a less flattering one than you would
have wished to hear? . . . Well, to suppose 'twere as
you say, you will grant me that the lot of our departed
friends would be one to wring our hearts when we

heard it recounted, calling forth our most charitable sympathy.—'Is there nothing we can do for the poor souls?' we should cry. And the world would answer 'Surely:—we can wear black for them: we can shut ourselves up in our own chambers; for a few months, we can refuse to go to any of the neighbours' houses; we can go nowhere except to church.'—This we can do, and we can do nothing more.

Isa. It is a sad reflection.

Will. Wait a bit;—wait a bit. I have only told you what the world says;—I say you *can* do more.

Isa. In what way?

Will. In this. You may mourn for a departed friend, not only according to the outward forms prescribed by a selfish world, but inwardly in your heart as well.—Before all else, you can *remember him*—cherish his memory. So you would not look to Time to dry your tears;—nor seek a refuge from your sorrow in Forgetfulness. No! for forgetting would be treason to your dead. But his image would be ever in your thoughts—his name often on your lips. In your daily converse you would cease to shun it—as 'twere some grim *memento mori*, which must send a shudder through the hearer. For you would have no fear but this:—that he whose face was lost to your eyes, whose voice had died away upon your ear, should be lost to your heart as well. For if he be lost to that, then is he lost indeed!

Isa. Ah me!

Will. Could you not think of him as of one whom you still might please, gone though he were, as you pleased him when by your side? You were then acquainted with his every wish:—is it, think you, so wholly un-availing to remember those wishes now?

Isa. (*rising*). O William, William! your words are rousing thoughts in my breast which have lain asleep till now;—mournful and cruel thoughts they are, mournful and cruel; as sad as time gone never to return, and cruel as the grave itself!

Will. (*rising*). Give these thoughts welcome, Isabel; make haste to afford them entertainment! They are late guests;—they have slumbered long; but, I tell you, 'twill be longer still or they sleep again.—Women there have been, child, who have been faithful to the man they loved *in spite of death !*

Isa. Some such there may have been; but they are few.

Will. Yes, they are few; they are few, indeed. Alas, and woe is me!

Isa. (*weeping, and wringing her hands*). What shall I do! what shall I do!

Will. Nay, do not weep. Never think that I cry alas! over any woes of mine. All that is past. I bewail the woes of Humanity.—That all is fleeting; all is, and must be, perishing—this is the bitter curse of Adam's race !—We see Joy fade; Love die; all that is bright and lovely pass away.—So let it be; in God's name, so let it be;—we are resigned.—But Sorrow; what of Sorrow? This is no benignant gift to be snatched from me like the rest. Here, surely, I may be constant, persevere. In Sorrow, surely—though neither in Love nor Joy—I may abide; and with constancy prove that I am more than the frail creature of an hour?—Alas! not so. Neither in Sorrow is there any endurance: it passes like the rest.—Yes, we are but children, children every one of us;—we cry ourselves to sleep to-night, and to-morrow waken with a smile. Alas! and again I cry alas, for poor Humanity! For Sorrow, our forlorn hope, is counted with the spoils of Time!

Mrs. M. (without). Where is he;—where is he? Take me to my son!

Will. My mother's voice!

Isa. I will leave you.   [*Exit.*]

Will. Mother!

[*Enter* Mrs. Mar.]

Mrs. M. William!

Will. Mother!

Mrs. M. My son! my son!

Will. Hush, hush! Be calm—for God's sake, be calm.

Mrs. M. Yes, yes! But, O William, O William, I never thought to see you again !

Will. Dearest mother.

Mrs. M. I thought you were drowned. I thought the sea had got you in its clutches and hidden you from me for ever.

Will. No, no.

Mrs. M. No, no—that was what I believed.—Ah, my son ! I have suffered upon your account.

Will. There is no need to tell me that.—Sweet mother, Sorrow is a hard master ; but I can see that you have served him well; for already he has invested you with those grievous badges of which his most faithful followers are the only wearers. Your poor cheeks are worn since I kissed them last . . .

Mrs. M. Ay; worn with tears.

Will. And your bonnie black braids are grey.

Mrs. M. Ah, yes; I 'm an old woman ! . . . But what of that—since I have you back again ?—You know grief will age one faster than years; and I have come through much. There have been times when I scarce knew what I did.—When the story of your drowning first reached me, I acted strangely.

Will. How so ?

Mrs. M. I 'll tell you. For a time I was stunned ; but that did not last; and then my affliction seemed heavier than I could bear. And casting about for succour in my

misery, I bethought me of the power of prayer. So I
went upstairs to my own room, and fastened the door,
and knelt down at the bedside.   But I must have been
beside myself; I could not pray.   My heart was hard;
and in the bitterness of my spirit, I cried aloud . . . and
what do you think I said?

Will. I cannot tell.

Mrs. M. I remember the very words.—I said, 'May
the winds never cease to vex the sea; nor the ships to
go to pieces on the rocks; nor seamen in extremity upon
the deep to cry to Heaven for help, and cry in vain; till
my dear son comes back to me in his likeness as I
knew him of old!'   And that was the only prayer my
lips would frame.

Will. O mother! those were rash and impious
words—words for which you might be punished.—Fie!
what made you speak like that?   It was wrong and
wicked of you.

Mrs. M. Forgive me, Will.   It was wrong;—but I
hope my punishment is past.   You do not know what
it is to suffer as I have suffered;—God grant that you
never may!

Will. Amen to that!

Mrs. M. Night after night, in my sleep, my son, I
have beheld you in deadly combat with the Sea.—I
have seen you try to beat it back;—but the Sea was
stronger than you.   You struggled, manfully, desper-

ately;—but the Sea was stronger than you.—I saw your arms beat faster and faster . . . but what could you do against such a foe, my boy, my babe that I nursed?—Then I saw that your strength began to fail, that you were well-nigh spent;—but the Sea was fresh and mighty as at first, like a giant at play with a child.—And then I heard you shriek—I heard you shriek to me! Think of it, my son; I heard you shriek to me, and I could not fly to help you . . . I covered my face.—And when I looked again, I saw the Sea, the hungry Sea; the cruel monster Sea :—his white fangs gleamed in the dark; his hundred heads were flung to the sky : I saw the Sea . . . but my son I saw no more.

Will. Poor mother!—But why recall your sufferings now?—It is useless, and only distresses you.—Come; you have me back again to-night. You must forget your sorrows. You must forget all your sorrows, to-night, mother, if 'tis only to welcome me home.

Mrs. M. So I will.—You are right;—it is foolish to talk of sorrow now, for my troubles are all at an end.

Will. So it seems; and yet, be not overmuch carried away by joy either.

Mrs. M. Nay, that caution is not needed. From to-night I bid good-bye to Grief—a long good-bye—and cast in my lot with Happiness for the future!—My boy, I've given ye but a sorry welcome,—but, remember, that had it been cheerier it would have been that I loved you less.

Will. Come, then, dry those tears.

Mrs. M. They are tears of joy, and therefore easily dried.—And, now I think of it, Will, of all nights i' th' year, 'tis the very best and fittest that you have chosen for your return.—You rascal! why, I believe you waited for it.—You know what night it is?

Will. Yes; Christmas Eve.

Mrs. M. Yes; Christmas Eve;—and you're come home, as a good son should, to spend it with your mother.—As our custom is, the neighbours and work-folk are assembled here:—they will be overjoyed to see you—poor souls; and think of their astonishment. They are at supper. Come; I'll tell you what I'll do:— I'll go tell them that there's a stranger here—a stranger from a distant country;—and then I'll present you.

Will. Ha!

Mrs. M. And you shall take your place at the head o' the table, and all shall drink to your health.—Remain where you are.   [*Exit* Mrs. Mar.]

Will. (*to himself*). A stranger from a distant country! Poor mother! she loves her jest.

[Mrs. M. *reappears in the doorway and beckons.*]

Lead the way!

[*Exeunt. A commotion is heard in the Supper-room.*]

[*Enter* CUTHBERT. *His manner exhibits a marked change from the elation of the earlier scenes.*]

Cuth. My place is taken! My place at the table is taken . . . my place in life is taken!—I am no longer the man I was. An hour ago I was Cuthbert Mar, Esquire of Windy Walls . . . now, I am Cuthbert Mar. Ah, times are changed indeed!' [*He seats himself and falls into a reverie.*] There's a certain growth, sprung from a tiny seed dropt long ago in fertile soil, that has been pushing blindly upwards for many years, that has reached the light to-night. . . . We were boys together—the rich brother and the poor:—the one, frank and winning, full of confidence in himself and all the world: the other, moody and shy;—so that need was all the world observed the contrast, and praised the elder for his generous spirit and open nature, whilst they passed the younger by unnoticed, or would remark that 'there was something not quite straightforward about him.'—'Something not quite straightforward about him,' forsooth! But it is never too early to begin to pay court to the rich,—to begin to slight the poor.—Did not I love to be spoken fair? Had I no relish for praise? Did not I prize the good word of the world . . . ? That's neither here nor there:—the world denied me. The world must share in the blame if I am what I am.—In those days I'd a friend—my father: my father; my brother's step-father.—

My father had been a fortunate man—at least in the last years of his life. A shipwrecked seaman, cast destitute on these shores, he had won the heart of the rich widow—my mother that was to be—and married her. It has been cast in my teeth that little was ever known of his history, or whence he came. But it seems that at least he had not always been well-to-do;—he knew the value of wealth too well. It was his dream to pass on what he now enjoyed to me, and leave me a rich man at his death. No doubt 'twas kindly meant of him, poor man;—but (Heaven preserve us from our friends!) there are some men more to be feared in their kindness than others in their cruelty.—I remember my father's policy:—how, when mother's back was turned, he would seize the opportunity to glorify in my brother's hearing the calling which had so near proved fatal to himself, and encourage Will's love for the sea; and how, if ever there was a difference to be made between us two, he would never see his own brat come off worst, not he! . . . My father died; and my brother and I grew up to man's estate. And here our paths divided. Hitherto we had been equals—bred up side by side; sharing alike in all advantages :—henceforth we were no longer such. The money was my brother's;—*he* was free—free to gratify his desires, to labour for the ends which seemed to him worth attaining, boundlessly free:—*I* was a slave. And the bitterness of slavery

I comprehended to the full. For, in my youthful dreams, I had fancied that within me which, in a world where native worth should outweigh mere accident of fortune, would have sufficed to lift me high. For good or ill, it was my faith that I was no ordinary man . . . Well! I found myself condemned, as if I were a felon, to hard labour for life—to that labour without inspiration whose sole end and aim is bread.—It was hard; but hard though it might be, I was prepared to face it. A poor man at the outset, I could have borne to live a poor man to the end. For it is not in being a beggar that the sting lies;—but to be made rich as I was by the turn of Fortune's wheel—and by rich, Heaven knows I do not mean in wealth alone—and to be made poor again, as I am made poor to-night, 'tis there's the outrage!— Oh, a curse upon the whole preposterous history! A curse upon my mother's passion! on my father's ill-judged fondness! on my brother, and this trick he's served me! on my own ambitious soul!—Banefully have they combined against me to make of me the sport of Fate.—For as I now stand here, stript of my short-lived greatness, hurling my vain invectives against Heaven, what am I so much as a spectacle to move laughter in gods and men?—a mockery to the Powers on high— the Envious Powers whose delight is in the thwarting of mortal schemes, in the dwarfing of human achievement;—and a laughing-stock to the outrageous mob

below, who have ever found in the misfortunes of
their fellow-creatures the source of their sincerest
satisfaction! Oh, I know them;—I know their mean,
market-going souls to the bottom! As like as not,
at this very moment, my downfall is the standing
jest at the supper-table. What more natural? They
have been paying honour where honour was not
due; they have discovered their mistake,—they take
their revenge.—So be it : but I fancy they none of 'em
know the man with whom they've got to deal. The
worm will turn ;—and Heaven knows I am no worm.
I 've submitted to Fate's ill-usage long enough. There
has long dwelt a devil within this breast; and he is
roused at last to-night! I boasted just now that I was
no ordinary man ;—I 've a mind to prove my words true.
—My brother? And what sort of brother has he shown
himself? A kind one? Ay, in his speech ;—but an
unkind in his dealing. His spoken words, I grant, have
been fair enough ;—but his unspoken words? ' *I take
the good things, which are my birthright ;—take thou the
evil, which are thine !*' And 'tis the unspoken words are
the weighty ones,—'*I take the good things which are my
birthright, brother ;—take thou the evil, which are thine :*'—
the world must be grown old indeed when brotherhood
is come to this . . . but no! I am forgetting. From
the beginning there was jealousy between brothers,
—jealousy, hatred, and strife :—jealousy, hatred, and

strife there shall be to the end . . . and the victory to
the strongest.

And now, a truce to moralising! In the first place, I
require an instrument—a cat's-paw. Where shall I find
him . . . ? That's more than I can tell. And 'tis not
the first found who would answer my purpose either.
There's a serious difficulty to start with . . . Now
were there but some Spirit (by whatever name he might
be known) such as I have heard of in old tales, who,
lost to grace himself, found consolation in such acts as
this I contemplate—would not he befriend me now?
The time and place chime well: and 'twere surely a
glorious opportunity, to assist into the daylight of Performance a deed still struggling between life and death
i' the dark womb of Purpose—a deed after his own
heart; and to win to his faction one whom life has left
a neutral, binding him to it with iron bands for ever!

[*A chuckle heard without.*]

[*Enter* SOLOMON.]

Cuth. The natural . . .

Sol. (*without seeing Cuthbert*). Haw, haw! I've stole
away to eat my Christmas pie by the kitchen fire.
The lads was beginnin' to pester me, as usual;—and,
besides, I can allus enjoy a Christmas pie best when I
be by mysel'.

Cuth. (*to himself*). They say the devil's children

have the devil's luck . . .—(*Aloud.*) How now, Solomon!

Sol. (*startled*). Cuthbert . . . murder!—I'd best get out o' 's way. [*Going.*]

Cuth. Hi, stop! where are you off to?—Stay. Come here; I want to speak to ye.

Sol. Yes, Maister.

Cuth. Why, man! what's the matter? You're not afraid of me, are you?

Sol. Yes, Maister.

Cuth. Yes!

Sol. I mean—no.

Cuth. Oh, you mean no;—that's right.—I'm sure you've no cause to be afraid o' me, Sol. I am your friend.

Sol. Eh?

Cuth. I say, I am your friend. I don't like to see the chaps ill-use you—I never did;—and if I were master here I would not allow it. I call it a shame.

Sol. A shame! ay, that it be.

Cuth. A damn'd shame.—And now tell me why you are not with the others rejoicing over William's return?

Sol. Ugh! What call have I to rejoice over his return?

Cuth. (*to himself*). Hum! Here's mule as well as ass, or I'm mistaken.—(*Aloud.*) Not much, 'tis true. —(*Tentatively.*) William was often hard on you . . .

Sol. No, 'a worn't.

Cuth. What the deuce d'ye mean, then?

Sol. 'A was never hard on me but once . . . but that once I shall never forget—no, not if I live to be a hundred!

Cuth. (*aside*). So-ho! I fancy I shall sail wi' the wind here.—(*Aloud.*) Why, he must ha' used you cruel bad indeed, Sol?

Sol. I b'lieve ye, zur.

Cuth. What did he do?

Sol. Will I tell 'ee?—Well: 'twere more 'n a year agone, one evening when t' lads was off work and hangin' about the doors wi' their hands i' their pockets, as I chanced to pass by. The little chaps what scare birds was a-following at my heels, a-calling of me wicked names, and singing,

> *' Simple Simon*
> *Met a pie-man,'*

and I dursn't turn on 'em, 'cause o' the others as was looking on.

Cuth. I see.

Sol. Well, up comes Will. And as soon as he catches sight o' me, says he, 'Now, lads, who's for sport?'

Cuth. For sport.

Sol. 'I'll tell you what,' he says. 'You all shall be a pack o' hounds; and Sol here shall be hare, and

you shall hunt en. .And, look 'ee here, if 'a shows
you any of his stubbornness, and don't lead you a right
chase from now till supper-time, you have my leave to
toss 'n in a blanket!'

Cuth. Dear me!

Sol. Wait a bit. The lads was game;—and so,
sore again' my will, I had to run, and they chevied me
—for all the world like a pack o' devils.

Cuth. Too bad, upon my word!

Sol. Stop a bit. I ran, Maister, ran for my life;
but, run as run I might, they'd ha' catch'd me long
afore supper-time. Well; they marched me back, and
fetch'd a blanket;—and, thof I begged and prayed of
'em to let me off, they in with me into un and tossed
me.

Cuth. A dangerous trick.

Sol. That is just what I said at the time. But you
ha'n't heard the worst of it yet.—Well they'd ha' tossed
me I know not how often, when Will, who was at the
window all the while a-laughing fit to split his sides,
cries, 'Now, lads, a good one for the last!'—And what
do you think they did? (Oh, 'twas a cruel trick to play;
—it makes me ill to think of un now!) They toss'd
me higher than ever, and then—would ye believe it,
Maister? instead o' catching me, the blackguards lets me
fall . . .

Cuth. Let you fall?

Sol. Ay ;—slap into the middle o' t' great holly-bush, all among the prickles !   . .

Cuth. Well ! all I can say, Sol, is that I wonder you 're alive to tell the tale.

Sol. I wonder at it myself ! My clo'es was tore, and my face and hands was scratch'd that they bore the marks for weeks arter.—'A gied me a crown the next day, did Will ;—but 'a might ha' gi'en me five and 'twould not ha' made up to me for all I had gone through ! No, it would not.

Cuth. I believe you. A joke 's a joke ; but that was going too far.—(*To himself.*) So ; the game 's fairly opened : now to play my cards with judgment.—(*Aloud.*) It has often surprised me, Sol, that a lad of your mettle should submit tamely to be treated as they treat you . . . ?

Sol. Anan ?

Cuth. In simple English, I 've often wondered that it has never entered your head to pay your tormentors out ?

Sol. Why, so it have. Often and often have I thought upon 't, and longed for the chance ;—but what can a pore boy do ?

Cuth. Poor boys have done much before now.

Sol. They 're all against me—every one !

Cuth. That may be ;—but luck has favoured you.— Listen, Sol. You 've a splendid chance to-night of paying your old tormentor out.

Sol. Eh ? my old tormentor ;—which of 'em ?

E

Cuth. Why, my brother Will, to be sure !

Sol. Tchk . . . ! without being found out ?

Cuth. Without being found out.

Sol. Certain sure ?—Tchk ! then at last I got my wish.
—O Maister ! I've longed for such a chance day and
night . . .

Cuth. And now it's come.

Sol. (*overjoyed*).   Tchk ! tchk !—Tell us how to set
about 'n.

Cuth. Hum . . . I'm not sure about that : I've a
mind to leave you that to discover.

Sol. Ay ! now, dawn't 'ee say that.   That would be
too bad o' you, it would—after tellin' a pore boy so
much.—Hark 'ee, zur.   For years 't has been my dream
to get a chance at one of 'em—a sly chance ; and I
thought 'twould never come.

Cuth. Never was there such a chance before ; never
will there be again.

Sol. Oh ! tell us what 'tis, Maister.   Come ; tell us
like a noble gentleman.

Cuth. Well ! Sol ; there's no resisting ye . . . Listen
to me.   (SOL *nods.*)   A year ago . . . d'ye remember
what happened a year ago ?

Sol. (*scratching his head*).   A many things.

Cuth. Exactly ;—one of which concerned my brother.
On the night we saw him last, he . . . got into a
scrape . . . d'you remember ?

Sol. So 'a did.

Cuth. . . . a scrape with the Coastguard. And, for a long time afterwards they were after him, searching high and low.

Sol. I mind.

Cuth. But at last, believing him dead, they gave up the search.—Now, Sol, don't you think that if the Coastguard knew that the man they were after was still in the land o' the living, they would be after him still?

Sol. I do believe they would.

Cuth. So do I.—Well, it just occurred to me that it would be a splendid trick—ha, ha! for any one who might have a bit of a grudge against Will . . .

Sol. Just so . . . ?

Cuth. Who might wish, in short, to pay off old scores . . .

Sol. To pay off old scores, that's it.

Cuth. That it would be a splendid trick, to go—without breathing a word to living soul, and before your man suspects his danger . . .

Sol. Yes, yes . . .

Cuth. To go to the captain of the Coastguard . . .

Sol. Ah . . .

Cuth. . . . and to tell him *that he had been too hasty in giving up the search, and where the man he sought is to be found.*

Sol. I understand 'ee, zur . . . hooray!

Cuth. It is but turning the tables upon Will, no more.

He set the plough-boys on to chase *you*, you say? well, you would be setting the King's men on to chase *him*. 'Sol shall be hare!' said he that night a year ago :— 'Will shall be hare!' say you to-night.

Sol. Ha, ha, ha! Capital.

Cuth. That's what we call paying a man back in his own coin, ain't it?

Sol. 'Tis so, and no mistake. 'Sol shall be hare!' said he yon night a year ago ;—and 'Will shall be hare!' says I to-night—ha, ha!

Cuth. Capital!

Sol. A splendid trick, to be sure.

Cuth. Splendid!—And now, if you've a mind to play off this splendid trick, you have no time to lose.—You know the Coastguard's quarters?

Sol. Ay ; white house on t' cliff.

Cuth. Exactly! Captain Derrick and his men will take their ease to-night :—you must go at once.

Sol. (*taken aback*). What, now . . . to-night . . . in the snow?

Cuth. Yes, now—at once. If ye don't go now, 'tis no use your going at all.

Sol. Bless us . . . ! But you would never have me go in the dark, Maister?

Cuth. By no means. You must take a lanthorn :— I'll light one whilst you make ready.

[*He proceeds to do so.*]

Sol. Oh . . . ! but 'tis a weary long way to the Rev'nue officer's house . . .

Cuth. A mere nothing to a pair of stout legs like yours.

Sol. And . . . I be afear'd to travel it alone, and at these timeless hours o' the night!

Cuth. (aside). Blast his fears!—(*Aloud.*) Afraid, Sol? why, what on earth is there to be afraid of?

Sol. I 'll tell 'ee. (*Whispers.*) Bogles, Maister Cuthbert; bogles and spirits!

Cuth. Stuff, Solomon! stuff and nonsense.

Sol. But remember . . . the road do lie by the Three Lane Ends, where Jacky Spratt as cut his throat lies buried.

Cuth. What then?

Sol. Why, an the gossips' tales be true, strange sights ha' been see'd there after dark.

Cuth. Pshaw! a parcel of lies; a parcel of lies invented by the old wives a' purpose to scare ye on night errands. You shall see nought more dreadful than your own shadow, Sol, that I 'll warrant ye.—Come, now;—sharp 's the word;—allow me to assist you . . . [SOL *is reluctantly fumbling with his choker;* CUTHBERT *takes it out of his hands and ties it for him.*] There!

Sol. But I dursn't pass the spot—indeed I dursn't!

Cuth. Now, look ye here, Sol; I am one who stands no nonsense.—Is it your wish to play off this splendid trick upon Will, or is it not?

Sol. Oh . . . yes, it is, but . . .

Cuth. It *is ;* that's enough for me : but me no buts, if you please.—It is your wish :—well, I'm resolved that you shall have your wish. I tell you I'm sick of seeing you submit tamely to be bullied—as if you hadn't the spirit of a mouse :—and I don't intend that you shall do so any longer. D'ye hear me?

Sol. Yes, Maister Cuthbert.—P'r'aps if I was to shut my eyes and run when I be near Jacky Spratt, I might get by un safe.

Cuth. Of course! You've but to whistle and keep a stout heart—there's nought will harm ye. And you'll have company on the way back. (*Sticks a cap on* Sol's *head.*) Now be off!

[Sol *makes a false start.*]

Sol. Oh! but I had forgot the Lone House—the lone house where Farmer Flayflint dwelt, the miser what died without ever making known where's treasure was hid; they do say 'a walks o' nights.

Cuth. Fiddlestick! that ghost was laid long since. At any rate I've told you, Sol, that I intend that you shall go upon this errand;—and I'm beginning to lose patience. So you may take your choice between Farmer Flayflint's ghost, which (so far as I could hear) was never yet known to give anybody such a cowhiding as he never had in his life before, and me!

Sol. I'm off, Maister; I'm off! I have got the spirit

of a mouse, han't I? and you'll stand by me, won't you? I'll run all the way.

Cuth. Ay, do; for the sooner you get there the better. (*Thrusts the lanthorn into his hand and sets the door open.*) See! the worst of the storm is past; the snow has ceased, and the wind has swept the heavens clear: you'll have a moon to light you on your way. I declare I almost wish I was going with ye my-self!

Sol. Oh, how I wish you were!

Cuth. Well, now be off!

Sol. Yes, Maister Cuthbert; I be going as fast as I can . . . Oh, you'll hold the door open till I be out o' sight?

Cuth. Yes, yes; I'll hold the door open; never fear! Think what a trick you're going to serve 'em;—and *remember the consequences if you fail.* Now, begone without another word!

Sol. Good-bye, Maister Cuthbert . . . It'll be a splendid way to serve un out, won't it? Good-bye, Maister Cuthbert; I shall soon be back . . . [*Exit.*]

Cuth. Good-bye: God-speed! (*He remains standing by the door.*) So; there he goes at last!—And now, my brother, I believe your bolt is sped. Ha, ha! you thought to take my place, did ye? Not so fast;— you've reckoned without your host this time, or I'm deceived. 'Tis not *my* place you shall take, man—not

mine, but another's!—Up on the High Moor, there's
a certain spot which timid folks avoid. It is a lodging
for but one man at a time—free quarters, too, and no
reckoning to pay. And, though the up-putting is rough,
no man grumbles at the hardness of that pillow; none
has need of a sleeping-draught to slumber the next
morning long after the sun is up.—The man who fills
this queer lodging to-night was a travelling tinker. He
begged of a poor woman at a cottage door, and, after
eating his fill of her charity, when her back was turned
set upon her with the knife . . . But the officers of
justice were too much for him : they 'tucked' him up;
—and there he hangs to this day. At first they kept a
watch upon his body, and then they kept a watch upon
his bones—lest friends should steal 'em away. But, by
this time, the birds have picked 'em clean :—he has
occupied his lodging long enough, and I think 'tis high
time he should clear out and make room for some one
else.—What think you, brother Will, of such quarters
for winter weather—you, who have kept me out i' the
cold so long? Upon blustering nights like this, one
can fancy that the gibbet creaks, creaks, as the wind
blows; and the wild creatures, lovers of the darkness,
steal round about; and the moon looks down out of
heaven . . . and hides her face.—Well! we shall see.
(*Closes the door.*) So, Solomon, speed upon your way.—
The next hour or two will be an anxious time; but,

that once safely past, I think I see myself once more a wealthy man, once more the Master of Windy Walls, once more the favoured suitor of Isabel!—Coraggio! what says the saw ?—

> ' *He either fears his fate too much,*
> *Or his deserts are small,*
> *That dares not put it to the touch*
> *To gain or lose it all!'* [*Exit.*]

ACT II.

SCENE: *as in* ACT I.

[*Enter* PRUDENCE *and* JACK.]

Jack (*sings*).—

' *Your Mol-ly has ne-ver been false, she declares,*
Since last time we par-ted at Wapping Old Stairs,
When I swore that I still would con-tin-ue the same,
And gave you the 'bacco-box mark'd with my name . . . '

Prue. Jack, Jack! I dunnot like to hear thee sing.— You was never used to do it except you was . . .

Jack. Call it 'three sheets in the wind,' lass.—Well! if I be three sheets i' the wind to-night, 'tis all along o' you.

E *

Prue. Along o' me?

Jack. I swear 'tis all along o' getting back to ye again, my dear; and being so glad to see 'ee.

Prue. A pretty way of showin' it!

Jack. Think how long it is since we last met . . . Nay, don't be snappish, Prue.—Come, my rosebud, sit by my side; give us a light to my pipe, and let 's ha' a look at ye.

Prue. Hey! not I.

Jack. Why, Prue, my dear, d' ye know what do astonish me is to see how well you wears.

Prue. Have done.

Jack. I declare now, that to look in your face fair calls to mind the days when I courted you.—D' ye mind them times . . . ? Ye do now, I 'll be sworn!

Prue. Indifferent well.

Jack. Ay, ay! a fancy-looking piece you was; and lightly would ye skim across the grass when the lasses an' lads played Kiss-i'-the-Ring on Goose Green on a holiday!

Prue. Ah! you was a rantipole then if ever was. My word! but ye made good the old sayin' that a sailor gets his money like a horse, and spends 't like an ass.

Jack. Ha, ha!—I say Prudence; d'you mind the Sunday afternoons when I would take 'ee out to walk? My stars! how fine ye would make yourself o' those Sunday afternoons!

Prue. I was young and fullish then.

Jack. And us 'ud walk out arm-in-arm—and you would answer all I said to ye, oh, so mim and so correct ! —Who would ever ha' guessed, my dear, as you 'd a voice might be heard a sea-league off in a gale o' wind, —and a tongue as must be slung by the middle, for I 'll swear 'a wags at both ends !

Prue. Ye took precious good care to gi' me no cause for using it then, Jack; for if ever a man was foolish-gone in love, that man was you. (JACK *winks.*)

Jack. And then, when us came to the sea-banks, you would first make me make sure as t' ground was dry, and would not soil your finery; and then we took a seat . . .

Prue. Ay ;—and you spun me yarns about furrin' countries, and mermaids, an' the sea-sarpint, an' the King o' the Cannibal Isles, and Lord knows what.

Jack (*aside*). And she believed 'em, bless her heart ! —(*Aloud.*) Ay ; and then I would begin to 'ee with, ' I say, Prudence . . . ' and you would answer me, ' Well, John ?'—And says I, ' I am but a rough-and-ready sailor-chap . . . ' And then you would look upon the ground, you would; and, says you, ' I likes a sailor.'—' But I don't think as you thinks much o' *me*,' says I.—' Indeed, but I *do*,' says you . . .

Prue. Never !

Jack. ' I think a very great deal o' you indeed !' Oh

you said it a score o' times if you said it once.—Ay, Prudence, you was fond o' me, you was!

Prue. I made 'ee think so.

Jack. Well, you've no call to be ashamed of it, my girl;—you only showed your taste. For as smart a little chap as you need wish to see was I when I brought up alongside o' you.

Prue. They say there's nowt like a good opinion o' yourself, at any rate.

Jack. Well, at last the happy day arrived—'twas not ong either;—trust Jack for coming quickly to the point—and a day it was!

Prue. You tied me a true-lover's knot with a blue ribbon . . .

Jack. And you wore it to church, you did, pinned over your bosom.

Prue. Ay, ay! Ours was something like a wedding, Jack;—believe me, you will scarce see the like of it to-day. For times be changed, and the young folks nowadays want sperrit.—'Twas a different thing when you and me was young.

Jack. True, true! folks understood better how to enjoy 'emselves.—For instance; after our wedding, there was none o' your leaving a trifle to be drunk at t' Public, and going quietly home . . .

Prue. I should think not. We'd music, we had; music and dancing, and sports o' every kind; races for prizes for the maids and wrestling for the lads ;—and to finish up the day, every man what owned a firearm kept a-letting it off i' the air as fast as ever 'a could load and load again ! It was splendid.

Jack. Splendid it was ! At the Sign o' the Horn of Plenty strong liquor flowed like water ; and there was neither man nor boy i' the parish walked straight to his bed that night.

Prue. For shame !

Jack. Well, after all, Prue, a man don't get spliced every day.

Prue. 'Tis as well for all consarned.

Jack. I won't say but what ye may be right there.— Ah, well ! Our wedding-day was a day to be remembered.

Prue. Now, they do say, Jack, as absence and salt water wash away love.

Jack. Never you believe 'em then, my dear, that's all ! It 's a lie—an invention o' the land-lubbers, as would serve Jack a scurvy turn behind his back ; it is, upon my soul !—And now, what do ye say to our drinking long life to faithful couples ? Oh, ye 've no need to be so missish, Prue ; you can go a little drop as well as another, I know ye can.—So come ; we 'll splice the main-brace to-night . . .

Prue. Well, well ! it ain't every night i' the year as Jack comes home.

Jack (as they go out).—

' *When I pass'd a whole fortnight be-tween decks with*
    you,
Did I e'er give a kiss, Tom, to one of your crew?
To be use-ful and kind with my Thomas I stay'd,
For his trow-sers I wash'd, and his grog too I
    made . . .'

[*Exeunt.*]

[*Enter* WILLIAM *and* MRS. MAR.]

Mrs. M. And now that I have you home again, my
boy, you must give me your word that you'll never
leave me again.

Will. They say Never's a long promise, mother.

Mrs. M. Not a day too long for me. O Will! can
it be that you have thoughts of leaving me already—you
who are but just come home?

Will. No, no; not yet.

Mrs. M. Not yet.—Ungrateful! and it is for this that
I have loved you dearer than my life . . . But, there!
you'll own that it is hard that all my love cannot win
you to give up the sea.

Will. Dear mother, why, you are not yourself to-
night.—Once a sailor, always a sailor, you know;—but
there's no need to speak so gloomily.

Mrs. M. No need . . . Oh! if Youth—Youth that
knows not its own cruelty—could but look for a moment

with the eyes of Age . . . . You are wrong, William :—I *am* myself to-night, if I never was before.

Will. I know you always bore a grudge against the sea, mother.

Mrs. M. Yes ; I hate the sea, and I fear it.

Will. And I love it.

Mrs. M. Ah, yes ! you did so from a child.

Will. I believe I did.

Mrs. M. And many an anxious hour you cost me even then.—I well remember a certain evening in those days, when you had not come home, and we were all gone out to look for you. Knowing your ways, I had gone straight to the shore, and was searching everywhere, calling you by name. At last, I came to the little church whose walls are washed by the waves ; and, peeping into the church-yard, there you lay ;—you were tired out with play, and had fallen asleep. I stood for a moment to look at you ; for then, as now, I could never feast my eyes on you enough. But, all at once I noticed that your little head was pillowed on a grave ; and on the headstone of the grave I read the words 'Perished at sea.' And when I looked about me, it seemed that every one of the stones bore the inscription, 'Drowned,' or 'Lost at Sea.'

Will. Ay, the coast hereabouts bears a bad name. We give it a wide berth when we can ; and seamen who ply the coasting-trade have christened it the 'Cemetery.'

Mrs. M. A feeling of foreboding came over me, and I

remember how I snatched you up and hastened home
through the gathering twilight, clasping you in my arms.
And from that day, I feared the sea for you . . .

Will. Surely, mother, you put no faith in such idle
fancies?

Mrs. M. Call them idle fancies if you will; I call them
by another name.—Is it unreasonable to believe that
where the fate of what we love best on earth is concerned, a foreknowledge of evil may be granted us?
No; they are no idle fancies, but the intuitions of a
mother's heart.—From that day, I feared the sea for
you; and sought, by all means in my power, to divert
your thoughts from it.   But, keep you indoors as I
would, I saw that your childish delight was still in build-
ing mimic vessels and in listening to sailors' stories.   I saw
it, and it made me sad and fearful.—Oh! how I strove
to win you from the sea at last.   But 'twas in vain.

Will. In vain!   A wilful man must have his way, ye
know, mother:—my heart was set upon the sea, and to
sea I went.

Mrs. M. In spite of me.

Will. No, no! but 'tis natural that a man should wish
to see the world;—you could not expect me to remain at
home all my days.

Mrs. M. I did not expect that.   And had you chosen
another calling—say, for instance, the soldier's—though
Heaven knows that there be bloody wars enough—I could

have bidden you go, and given you my blessing.   But I would have had you shun the sea.

Will. How like a mother ! 'tis the way they all deceive 'emselves.   For had it chanced to be the red coat instead o' the blue jacket that took my fancy, you know in your heart that you 'd ha' been as much against it.   [*She shakes her head.*]   But I 've never repented of my choice.   The sea-life is the life for me :—the wide world holds none like it !

Mrs. M. No, truly ;—none so full of dangers and hardships.

Will. None so roving ; none, spite all its rubs, so pleasant, or so free.

Mrs. M. None for wearing away with sorrow and anxiety the lives of those you leave behind.   But you never think of that.—Ah, Will ! what is it to you how often I have lain awake at night, listening to the storm and praying that my son might be preserved ?   What is it to you how often my eyes have filled with tears when I have looked from my window over the waters, when you were far away ?   And you know how, in all parts of this house, if you listen when the wind is still, you can catch the sound of the sea . . .

Will. (*listens*).   I hear it now.   One might fancy the alternate rise and fall of the waves to be the breathing of some heavy sleeper.

Mrs. M. To me it has a different sound.   Night and

F

day, idle and at work, I have heard it these many years ;
and, as its murmurs came to my ear again and again, I
have said to myself, ' *There is sorrow on the sea ;—there
is sorrow on the sea ; it will not be quiet.*'

Will. Fancies, fancies again, mother.

Mrs. M. Not so.   My boy, my boy ! believe me, there
is sorrow on the sea.

Will. And is there not sorrow on the land as well—
sorrow and change in hearts we fondly thought un-
changeable ? (*rising*) I have found it so . . .

Mrs. M. Poor boy !

Will. And I turn for consolation, for forgetfulness,
where I may.

[*Enter* CUTHBERT.]

Ah ! here comes Cuthbert.

Cuth. The clock has just struck midnight ;—it is
Christmas Morn.

Mrs. M. The season of peace on earth, and good-will
among men :—may its blessings, in rich measure, be
upon this house !

Will. So let it be.—Cuthbert, my lad, give us your
hand.   I was vexed with thee just now . . . But there !
As mother says, this is no season for ill-will—least of all
between brothers.   Let us be friends.   [*Music without.*]

Cuth. With all my heart ;—I wish for nothing better.
—(*Aside.*) He might have spared me that grasp of the
hand !   Taken together with the associations of the day,

it was suggestive of a certain *kiss.* Ah, well . . . ! [*He turns away.*]

[*Enter* ISABELLA.]

Isa. (*to* MRS. M.). I wish you a peaceful and a happy Christmas, aunt!

Mrs. M. Niece, your wish is bountifully fulfilled. May your Christmas, my dear girl, be as happy as is mine! More than that I know not how to wish you. [*She kisses her.*]

Isa. Where do you think I have been? At my window, listening to the carol-singers. The wind has fallen; and, in the stillness of the night, their singing sounded so sweet. It seemed almost like the music of angels.—You must hear them. [*Opens window.*]

Carol-singers (*without*).—

> ' *Hark! the herald-angels sing*
> *Glory to the new-born King,*
> *Peace on earth, and mercy mild,*
> *God and sinners reconciled.*
> > *Hark! the herald-angels sing*
> > *Glory to the new-born King.*'

Mrs. M. It is beautiful indeed, Isabel;—and indeed it brings to mind the song which, on this night ages ago, the Angel sang to the shepherds as they watched their flocks: ' *Behold, I bring you good tidings of great joy!* ' For, in truth, great joy is mine this night.

Cuth. (*aside*). Poor mother !—(*To* Mrs. M.) Mother, remember that great joy is mostly short-lived.—(*To* Isa.) Come ; the night air makes one shiver.

[Cuthbert *closes the window, which remains unshuttered.*]

[*Enter* Playfair.]

Play. (*to* Mrs. M.). Mistress, a Happy Chris'mas and a Good New Year to you ; and may God bless ye !

Mrs. M. Thank you, Playfair ; and the same to you.

[Play. *bows.*]

Play. In the other room the supper has gone off beyond a wish ; and, after eating and drinking every man his fill, the guests be about rising from table.

Mrs. M. We'll have them in, then.—But first, a word with you.

Play. At your commands.

Mrs. M. Listen.—This is no ordinary Christmas Eve, Playfair. To-night your Master, whom we had mourned as dead, is come back to his home once more ; to-night my dear and long-lost son is found ;—we must make it such a night as all here will remember. It is my wish.

Play. It shall be my endeavour.

Mrs. M. You will oblige me.—Let me consider . . . In the first place, let me have more lights here ; methinks the room is but dimly lighted ;—and then go round the house and blow the fires up to a warm and cheerful blaze.—And, look you, do not spare ; see that no man wants for anything. Plenty must reign at Windy Walls to-night . . . The Yule Log ! I trust you have provided a noble one; I want to see it blaze and crackle on the hearth and the flame roar up the chimney. And don't forget the Christmas Candle. And the Wassail Bowl—you must brew that strong, steward ! let me see the liquor bubble bravely ; ay, where you brewed it sweet and strong before, see you brew it three times sweeter, three times as strong to-night.

Play. It shall be done.

Mrs. M. And whoever praises your brewing, bid him drink long life and happiness, and a welcome home, to his Master, my sweet William.—And, Playfair, I remember of old what a famous hand you were at devising sports for the merry-makers. Be upon your mettle to-night, man—I ask it of you ; for I wish the whole house to share my happiness.

Play. Trust me, mistress ; they shall if I can make 'em.

Mrs. M. That's right.—Now call them in.

[*He goes.*]

[*Enter from the Supper-room* PRUDENCE, OLD HICKA-
THRIFT, JACK, DAVY, HOBNAIL, TOM TUCKER, *and
all the other Guests ;—hand-shakings and Christmas
greetings are being exchanged on all sides.*]

Mrs. M. Good folks ! a Merry Christmas to you all.

Several Guests. Same to you, Mistress; same to you, and many of 'em!

[MRS. MAR *drops a curtsey.*]

Mrs. M. (*to* PLAY.) Is the fiddler here?

Play. He is, ma'am.—Fiddler Anthony, step forward.

Mrs. M. (*to the* FIDDLER). Now, fiddler, I want ye to tell me what are your best and liveliest tunes?

Fid. Faith, Mis'ess Mar! there's '*God rest you, Merry Gentlemen,*' a lifey stave enow; or, an 't please ye better, there's the '*Roast-Beef o' Old England,*' '*When the King Enjoys 's Own Again ;*' or, ''*Tis My Delight on a Shiny Night,*' or, '*Hearts of Oak.*'—Or, I can gie 'ee '*With Jocky to the Fair,*' or, for t' matter o' that, '*Ower the Hills and Far Away,*' or, '*Bumper, Squire Jones !*' But, if 'tis the merriest measures I can play ye be enquirin' for, why, to make no bones about it, they be '*Drunk at Night and Dry i' the Morning,*' and t' '*Devil among the Tailors !*'

Play. Fie upon 'ee, fie upon 'ee, fiddler! would'st name them loose tunes to a lady?

Mrs. M. Well, well! I leave the choice of the airs to yourself. Only, hark 'ee now, if ever, let your music be in tune; and, if ever in your life you put spirit in your playing, do so to-night.

Fid. I'll do my best, ma'am.

Play. No man can do more.   [FIDDLER *retires.*]

Mrs. M. (catching sight of OLD HICK.). What, Hickathrift! I had not seen ye before to-night.—Why, how
well you are looking!

Old H. Ah, mistress! I be a old man.

Jack. But wonderful fresh of his years.

Old H. Well, I cannot complain, and that's truth.
Man and boy, I ha'e wrought upon this farm seven-an'-
fifty year; and never off work but a week and odd
days altogether.

Mrs. M. Do you say so!

Old H. 'Tis none so long ago, neither, as I could still
lend a hand to save hay, or in harvest-time.

Jack. There's a wonderful old man for ye, mistress.

Mrs. M. Indeed he is.

Old H. I take my meals well still.

Jack. Ay, and 'a would foot it to Kirk and back
reg'lar, o' Sundays.

Old H. But I be failin' at last, mis'ess; I be getting
hard up, hard up.

Jack. Nonsense, dad! I do b'lieve 'a's fresher
than when I last saw en.

Mrs. M. He certainly looks remarkably well to-night.
Ah, Hickathrift! this is a joyful night for you as well as
for me, for you too have a son that was lost come home.
Come! the couples are taking their places; you shall be
my partner in this country dance;—and we'll show
the young folks what the old ones can do!

Old H. Ah, Mis'ess Mar! my dancing days be over.

Jack. Not a bit of it, daddy; not a bit of it! Come, never refuse a good offer.

Mrs. M. I will not take a refusal—there. 'Tis many a year since I have danced myself, but to-night my heart's so light that dance I must. For it is—

> ' *Merrily danced the Quaker's wife,*
> *Merrily danced the Qua-ker !'*

Fiddler, strike up!

Davy. Scrape away.

Play. (*to* Davy). The mistress is like her old self again to-night, Davy;—it does a man's heart good to see her.

Davy. Ay, ay! 'tis a sight for sore eyes, and so it is.

Isa. (*to herself*). I trust they may be right; but I have never seen my aunt in such high spirits before, and I could wish that she were calmer.

Will. (*to* Cuth.) Come, Cuthbert, my boy, don't ye dance?

Cuth. (*declining*). Believe me, I had rather look on.

[*Music :—a country dance is performed.* Cuthbert *looks on in moody silence.*]

Play. (*as the dance comes to an end*). And now, souls, we've the night before us :—how shall we begin ?—But,

before ye answer me, is there e'er a lass here that's not
provided with a sweetheart? If there be, let her speak!
[*Laughter, accompanied by nudging and giggling among
the Guests.*] What, not one? Then what am I to do
myself? I see I shall ha' to fight some of ye. [*Renewed
laughter.*] And now, how are we to begin? Is it to be
a round game, or another dance? Come! who says
Hunt-the-Slipper, Snap-Dragon, Forfeits? who's for
Shoeing-the-Wild-Mare, Hot-Cockles, Turn-the-trencher,
or Blind-Man's-Buff?—When we be out o' breath, and
not before, we'll get it back behind a hand o' cards, or
with telling o' tales over the fire, and singing ballats an'
catches. And then, to wind up the night, we'll dive
for apples and jump for cakes an' treacle . . . But
the question o' the moment just now is, how we
begin?

Davy (*coming forward*). Mister Steward! the Guizards
be outside t' door, askin' leave to come in and perform.

Guests. The Guizards, the Guizards!

Play. (*to* MRS. M.). Have they your permission,
mistress?

Mrs. M. By all means.

[*Enter Four Maskers grotesquely attired to represent*
FATHER CHRISTMAS, *the* KING OF MACEDON,
GALASHON, *and the* DOCTOR.—*Amid a buzz of
anticipation, the Guests form a semicircle to*

look at the Play. MRS. MAR, ISABELLA, *and* WILLIAM *sit.*]

[THE PLAY.]

FATHER CHRISTMAS—
> *Redd stocks, redd stools,*
> *Here comes in a pack o' fools—*
> *A pack o' fools behind the door,*
> *Such fools were never seen before!*

Davy (aside). 'A never said a truer word !

A Guest. Haw, haw !

KING OF MACEDON—
> *Here comes in the great King o' Macedon,*
> *That conquer'd the world round and round !*
> *So stout and so bold,*
> *So frank and so free,*
> *I call upon Galashon*
> *To come and fight with me !*

Davy (aside to Guests). His name is Dicky Dean, when 'a's at home ; and his motto, ' Speed the Plough !'

> [*Laughter.*]

Play. Order, order ! turn him out.

GALASHON—
> *Here comes in Galashon,*
> *Galashon is my name . . .*

Will. (to ISA.). Ha, ha ! look at Galashon. 'Pon my life, he's been stealing from the scarecrows !

Isa. The Doctor's pigtail alone 's worth the money ;—
I hope you do it justice.

Mrs. M. Hush ! you naughty children, be quiet ;—
don't you see you put the creatures out.

Play. Come, speak up, Galashon !

GALASHON—

> *With sword and pistol by my side,*
> *I hope to win the game !*
> *My body 's like a rock,*
> *And my head is like a stone . . .*

Davy. True for you again !

GALASHON—

> *And I will be Galashon*
> *When you are dead and gone !*

KING OF M. *You, sir ?*

GAL. *Yes, I, sir !*

KING OF M. *Draw your sword and try, sir !*

> [*The* KING OF M. *and* GALASHON *draw swords*
> *and fight.*]

Cuth. (*during the combat, to himself, standing
apart*). By this time Solomon must have seen the
Officers, and they should be well on their way hither !
(*Glancing towards the Guizards and their audience.*)
Accident favours me. 'Tis plain that not one of these
poor simple souls has the faintest inkling of the mischief
that 's brewing—the smallest foreboding of the surprise

I have in store for 'em.—There they stand ;—and give themselves up to the ridicule of these pitiful clodpole merryandrews—exactly as though there were no such power as Evil for ever busy under the sun ! A curious spectacle.—And I, as I stand here and watch them— the spectre at the feast—am not I a very counterpart of Destiny herself? the spider, Destiny—the weaver of meshes delicate, but strong ; the omnipotent worker-in-the-dark ;—whilst these poor merry-makers may serve me for the type and epitome of eternally short-sighted Man.—My brother laughs with the loudest of 'em ; lounges and laughs ; laughs the precious moments away !—Laugh, then ;—laugh on ;—laugh while you may ! You will not laugh long.—My plans are laid ; my puppets set in motion ;—I have no more to do. Time does the rest !—I am idle, and await the result.

> [*Toward the close of this speech the face of* Sol
> Meiklejohn *is seen outside the unshuttered
> window.—*Derrick's *face appears next ; then*
> Lobb's, *and, then, one by one, those of several
> others of the Coastguard.—They are seen to
> reconnoitre with caution ;—exchange some whispered
> communications, and then withdraw again.—In
> the meantime the Guizards' Play is proceeding
> as below, and the attention of the whole party
> indoors is absorbed in it.*]

[Galashon *wounds the* King of Macedon, *who falls.*]

GALASHON—

> *Alas, alas ! what's this I 've done?*
> *I've kill'd my father's only son !*
> *Around the kitchen and the hall,*
> *It is the Doctor that I call !*

THE DOCTOR—

> *Here comes in Beelzebub ;*
> *And over my shoulder I carry a club,*
> *And in my hand a frying-pan ;*
> *I think myself a jolly old man !*

FATHER C. *How far have you travelled?*

DOC. *From York to Cork.*

FATHER C. *Any further?*

DOC. *From knife to fork.*

FATHER C. *What 'll you take to cure this dead man?*

DOC. *Twenty pound and a bottle o' wine.*

FATHER C. *Would five do?*

DOC. *No ! five would not put on a good coal fire ; and if it did, the devil would come down chimbley and put en out.*

FATHER C. *Then cure this dead man at once.*

DOC. *This is a wondrous bottle called ' hoxy-croxy' :—*
> *I put a little to his head . . .*
> *A little to his leg . . .*

> [*Whilst the* DOCTOR *is bending over the* KING OF
> M., *enter* SOL *by door* C. *He steals up to*

CUTHBERT, *who still stands apart, and plucks him by the sleeve.*]

Sol. (*whispering*). Officers be come!

Cuth. (*without turning*). What's that to me?

Sol. (*whispering*). They be outside window; but they dursn't come in. They say there are too many i' the room; and they fear a rescue, and to get mauled by the work-folk for their pains.

Cuth. Ha!

Sol. One of 'em is for going away again.

Cuth. (*to himself*). That won't do . . . (*To* SOL.) Go back, Sol. Persuade the Officers to stay where they are and watch their opportunity. And bid them, as they value a whole skin, *lie close!* (SOL *nods assent.*)

[*Exit* SOL. *The Play proceeds.*]

DOC. . . . *Now, rise up, Jack, and fight again!*

KING OF MACEDON—

> *Once I was dead—*
> *But now I am alive;*
> *And blessed be the hand*
> *That made me to revive.*

CHORUS OF GUIZARDS—

> *There are four of us in all,*
> *And merry boys we be;*
> *And we are going a-rambling,*
> *Some houses for to see—*

Some houses for to see,
  And some pleasure for to have ;
And what you freely give to us
  We freely will receive.

God bless the Master of this house,
  The Mistress also ;
And all the little boys and girls
  That round the table go :
May your pockets be full of money,
  And your barrels full of beer ;
And we wish you a Merry Christmas,
  And a Happy Good New Year !

[*On the conclusion of the Play follows a storm of applause, during which* SOLOMON *re-enters and the Guizards exeunt.—As they go out* CUTHBERT *springs forward and leaps upon a table.*]

Cuth. (*boisterously*).   And now, good people, *I* have a game to propose !

Play. Hear, hear !   Mister Cuthbert's game.

Cuth. And, as it's a game in which all can join, except cripples and such as have been at the wars—I declare that whoever will not play shall pay me a forfeit forthwith !

Davy. D'ye hear that? all who won't play pay forfeits.

Cuth. My game is called, *Follow my' Leader ;*—and all the players have got to do is to follow wherever I may lead 'em, and whatever they see me do, to do the same !

Sol. (*chuckling to himself*). He's a clever un, he is.

Cuth. So, come! form up in line behind me in quick time—and off!

Jack. Hurrah! this is the game for my money. Come, Prudence, my girl, catch hold!

[*He places himself behind* CUTHBERT; PRUDENCE *follows him, and* DAVY, PRUDENCE, *and the Guests, entering uproariously into the fun, form themselves in single file in a tail behind, and seize each other by the skirts and coat-tails.*]

Sol. (*to himself*). Dash my wig if I be going to play! I knows where better sport is to be found.

Cuth. (*addressing his followers*). Now then;—all together;—at a steady double . . . forward!

[CUTHBERT *sets off at a jog-trot, and is followed by all the Guests except* PLAYFAIR, SOLOMON, *and* OLD HICKATHRIFT. *He first leads his followers a dance round the Kitchen—scrambling over benches, doubling on his track, and, as he passes under it, leaping up to touch the Mistletoe, but always carefully avoiding the neighbourhood of the Window.—While this is in progress :—*]

Mrs. M. (*to* WILL.). And now, my boy, in case you should be weary of all this uproar, and wish to slip away

and lie down, I will go look at the room I've had prepared for ye, and see that your bed is ready.

[*Exit* MRS. M. *by door* R.]

[*Having by this time led his followers two or three
times round the room,* CUTHBERT *all at once in-
creases his pace and makes for door* L.]

Cuth. (*as he reaches the door, shouting and waving his
hand*). Tally-ho—hark for'ard—gone away!

Jack (*imitating* CUTHBERT). Tally-ho—hark for'ard
—gone away!

Guests. Tally-ho . . . hark for'ard . . . gone awa-a-ay!

[CUTHBERT *now runs out at the door which leads
into the Supper-room; and the Guests follow
helter-skelter. As the last of them disappears, the
sash of the unshuttered window is noiselessly raised,
and* DERRICK *and* LOBB *enter through it.* LOBB
*quickly closes the window behind him and shuts the
shutters, while* DERRICK *springs to the door by
which the Guests have passed out, locks it, and
pockets the key.—Their actions are so swift, and
at the same time so silent, that their presence in
the room is not at once discovered.*]*

---

* *During the following scenes, in which* OLD HICKATHRIFT *and*
SOLOMON *take no part, the former sits in the chimney corner, alter-
nately spreading his hands over the fire, nodding drowsily and waking
up again—apparently indifferent to all that takes place; the latter
conceals himself from those on the stage and looks on.*

G

Isa. (*to* WILL.). That was a brilliant inspiration of Cuthbert's.

Will. Indeed it was! I never knew him put so much spirit into any game before.

Der. (*coming forward and presenting his warrant*). William Lee! I arrest you in the King's name.

Will. Eh? what's this . . . ?

Der. If you are a wise man, sir, you'll submit quietly; 'twill be best in the end for all parties. I may tell you that I have my crew with me, under arms; so no good can come of resistance. And as for any attempt at escape, it will be useless; for I've a man posted at every outlet to prevent it.

Will. (*bewildered, reading from warrant*). ' *Night of the 25th January*, . . *causing death of Revenue Officer*' . . . what, in the name of wonder, is all this?

Der. The charge. Is it your intention to deny it?

Lobb. A cool hand if 'a do,—what can be sworn to by a dozen o' eye-witnesses!

Will. Deny it . . . No . . . I fired the shot.

Der. Well . . . ! you're a marksman.

Will. What d' you mean?

Der. That you killed your man.

Will. Killed him! . . . O God!

[*A pause.*]

Isa. (*to* PLAY.). This will be a terrible blow to your mistress.

Play. Indeed, miss, I fear it will!

[*Re-enter from door* R, MRS. M.]

Mrs. M. Now, Will, your bed is ready for you ; and the fire in your room burns brightly. It's the old room, —the one you slept in as a boy.

Will. (*in altered tones*). Mother!

Mrs. M. William ! (*She catches sight of the Officers.*) Why, what's this? These men . . . who are they, and what's their business here?

Will. (*to* DER.). Speak for yourself.

Der. My name is Robert Derrick, of His Majesty's Coastguard; at your service, ma'am ;—and this is my mate. We are here on . . . a disagreeable errand.

Mrs. M. A disagreeable errand, eh . . . ? Ah! I felt it was too bright to last.—(*To* DER.) Well, what may your errand be? Disagreeable or not, let us hear it.

Der. I'm sorry ye should think it needful to compel me to speak more plainly . . . Did you understand me when I said I belonged to the Revenue Service?

Mrs. M. The Revenue Service . . . (*Recollecting.*) Then you've come for my son !

Lobb. That's about it.

Der. It is my duty to apprehend him.

Will. And their duty must be done, mother ;—there's no help for it.

Lobb. None in Christendom.

Mrs. M. (*to* WILL.). O William, William, how could you bring this trouble upon yourself and upon me?

Will. Well, mother, I acknowledge the thoughtlessness of my conduct; but I could not foresee the results. Regrets are worse than useless now.

Mrs. M. Only think how happy we were! We had everything that heart could wish, every blessing under the sun . . . and you must spoil it all—all for the sake of a few pounds, too, which we did not require.

Will. It was the excitement, not the love of money, that tempted me . . . However, when all's said, the fact remains that 'twas a rash and hare-brained business, and has cost more than one of us dear.—Oh, how I could curse my folly now! bitterly do I repent me of it . . .

Mrs. M. Yes; when it is too late: 'tis always so.

Will. Well, mother, I am punished—punished severely enough in all sadness, as it turns out.

Mrs. M. You don't know yet what your punishment will be . . .

Der. (*under his breath*). That's what I suspect the lady herself don't know, nor yet guess.

Mrs. M. But, after all, the penalties for contraband trading cannot be so very terrible; and your offence, I dare swear, was no very serious one. At all events, what's past's past cure, remember that;—and there's nothing to be gained by being so much cast down about it. So, cheer up, my boy! Let the Law do its worst: we're rich; we can afford to laugh at it. Whatever has to be paid for you shall be paid,—though the farm be sold to raise the money! Of that rest assured.

Will. Alas . . . ! But what if there be that to pay which the sale of the farm will not cover?

Mrs. M. Then we'll sell all we possess! I care not what we part with, or how little we keep, so long as I get you back. After all, what's ruin? a change of residence: what's poverty? a change of fare. And change is lightsome; I am fond of change! There's but one thing which I can't and will not bear; and that's to be parted from you.

Will. O mother! that's the very thing that you will have to bear.—Yes; we must part.

Mrs. M. Not, I hope, for long.

Will. (to Isa.). Either she does not know the worst, or she refuses to believe it. I must put an end to this. (*To* Mrs. M.). Dear mother; our trouble is far heavier than you think for . . .

Mrs. M. Ah?

Will. Yes; there is still more for that poor heart to bear, which has already borne so much . . . God help me!—Now, be calm; and try to recall the events of that unhappy night . . .

Isa. Yes, dearest aunt, remember.

Will. There was some one else, it seems, besides myself and Jack . . .

Der. Ay; that there was! the trouble ain't all o' your side, I can tell ye.   He was the best o' shipmates, was our late commander: as stout a seaman, too, as e'er faced the weather; and 'a leaves a widow and young family unprovided for.   Ay, my fine fellow! there 's work enough (and cruel work too, some o't) for the Coastguard, without you gentlemen starting as smugglers-for-pleasure.—You be suffering for it now; but you 've brought it upon your own head: and others, who were innocent, have suffered for your act.

Will. You 're a Job's comforter, my friend: still, your words are but too true;—and I 'm obliged to ye at least for one thing.—(*To* Mrs. M.) Mother, whatever happens, see you don't forget the widow and orphans. They are unprovided for: provide for them;—'tis the least we can do.—Remember, it is my last request.

Mrs. M. (*starting as if out of a dream*). What . . . ? (*No one replies.*) What?—(*Addressing herself to* Der-rick; *speaking rapidly.*) Officer! Speak . . . tell me the truth . . . my son is charged with causing that man's death?

Der. That is the charge.

Lobb. And 'a don't deny it.

Mrs. M. Ah! I had hoped against hope . . .—(*To* Der.)   But, tell me—I can't trust my own head; I 'm not myself to-night—tell me, I beseech you, how will they punish him?

Der. Hum . . . indeed, madam . . .

Mrs. M. Speak out! Can you not answer a simple question?

Der. Indeed, mistress, 'tis hard to say how they will punish him.—(*Aside.*) God forgive me!

Mrs. M. (*with violence*). It's a lie.

Will. Mother!

Isa. Dear aunt . . .

Mrs. M. Let me alone.—(*To* DER.) You're deceiving me.—(*To* LOBB.) You, sir. It's a plain question that I ask;—let me have a plain answer. What will be my son's punishment?

Lobb (*to* DER.). Best let her have her own way;— 'tis the only plan.—(*To* MRS. M.) Well, mis'ess, you're right: we do know what his punishment will be . . .

Mrs. M. Well . . .?

Lobb. In plain English,—the gallows.

[MRS. MAR *shrieks aloud.* WILL, *with a gesture of anguish on his mother's account, sinks down upon a seat and covers his face.*]

Isa. (*indignantly*). Barbarous man! Is it not enough to have brought this trouble upon us that you must insult us too?

Lobb. Easy there, miss! The trouble's none o' my

bringing ;—and, sooner or later, your relative must ha'
been told.

Mrs. M. Hist!—(*To* DER. *and* LOBB ; *she has regained
her self-possession*). Gentlemen, by your leave,—a
word.

Lobb. What is it now ?

Mrs. M. I 've a proposal to make :—I think I see a
way clear out of this difficulty, with satisfaction to both
you and me.

Der. You 'll lose your labour.

Lobb. Cut it as short as you please, then : remember,
our time is the King's.

Mrs. M. I will be very brief.—You come here to-night
for gain, gentlemen ;—gain you shall have. Name the
sum.

Der. Mistress !

Mrs. M. What 's wrong ? It is quite simple.—The
Government pay you, don't they, to take my son ? I 'll
pay you double, treble, to let him go free ! What 's the
figure ?—you know that what I promise in this respect
I can perform.

Lobb. (*uneasily*). Walls have ears . . .

Mrs. M. Don't fear for that ! Not a soul shall ever
hear of it; or, if any one do, I 'll buy him. Oh, I 'll
bribe, bribe, bribe . . . I 'll bribe the whole country-
side, if need be, to hold their tongues. The money 's
forthcoming . . .

Der. No doubt.—(*With decision.*) Now, mistress, once and for all, we cannot listen to that proposal : that would never do at all.

Lobb. No more it would !—The bird i' the hand's the bird for me.

Mrs. M. But, gentlemen . . .

Der. No more o' that ! I say I will not hear another word.

Mrs. M. Then I 'll say no more of that, I promise you; only hear me. You are honourable men ;—forgive my blunder ; and hear me speak to you as honourable men. —You come here to take my son . . . but, do you know our story? I cannot think you do.—He 's my eldest son, sir. A year ago I lost him, as I believed ; and I mourned for him . . . oh, how I mourned for him ! And to-night, this very night, he 's come back to me, safe and well. Think of my joy ! think of my joy at getting back a son whom I thought dead. Think of my joy, and you 'll never have the heart to take him from me again . . .

Der. We 've no choice : it is our duty.

Mrs. M. Duty? No ; you shall not plead duty ! duty this cannot be. Duty is something high and noble ; difficult to perform ; something which brings honour to the doer. So we speak of duty to parents, duty to God, duty towards our neighbour . . . and my duty to my neighbour is to love him as myself—ay, mark you that ;

and to do unto others as I would they should do unto me. Such is duty.—And you would call it your duty to come armed, by night, and tear a son from his mother's arms? Oh, you abuse the word; you abuse the word unworthily!

Der. I hope not, mistress: I hope I know my duty. My duty is to His Majesty the King,—to obey my orders. My duty's plain to-night.

Lobb. As a pike-staff.

Mrs. M. No, no! (*Distractedly, wringing her hands.*) My son! my lost William come home to-night . . . ! —(*Turning again to the Officers.*) Good sirs! you had mothers of your own;—think of them now. I, whom you see before you, am a mother—a mother even as they are.—Like them, long since, I rejoiced with exceeding great joy over the man-child that was born to me; like them I nursed him on my knee; like them watched him grow up . . . like them, perhaps, I have suffered since on his account.—Oh! think of your own mothers, think of them . . . and, by their memory, as you ever held it dear, hold sacred now the motherhood in me.

Lobb. It is no use.

Mrs. M. No use . . . ! Oh, shame on you; shame on you! Are you men? had you mothers of your own, and can you bear to use a mother as you are using me? See! I'm an old woman; my hair is grey—and grey hair

was once worthy of reverence; yet I go down on my
knees before you—I who never knelt to man before!

Play. That I should live to see the day!

Der. It is useless. I 'm sorry for you, mistress; but,
as I tell ye, I 'm not my own master.—Duty 's duty!

Lob. So it is, mate, all the world over! Our duty
has got to be done; and the sooner we set about it the
better. (*Turning to* WILL.) Now, master . . .

Mrs. M. (*throwing herself between them*). No! you
shall not lay a finger on him . . . not while I am
mistress here. Wild beasts will fight for their young,
and so will I—for you drive me to forget that I 'm a
woman.—Playfair! are you a man? and will you stand
quietly by and see your master dragged to his death?

Play. Not I! Master Will, we 're two to two . . .

Will. (*raising his head*). No, Playfair; I forbid it.

Mrs. M. (*excitedly*). But, Will, you forget; we 're not
alone: there are our Christmas guests—a score of stout
fellows on whose pluck we can rely, and every man of
'em ready to fight for you and me. Oh, what a blessed
chance that brought them here . . . . !

Der. Not so fast, if you please. Remember that if
you have your work-folk, mistress, I 've my crew. They
are close at hand; and a note on this whistle summons
them.

Mrs. M. Your crew . . . ? My men outnumber
them.

Lobb. Raw country louts.

Mrs. M. But they can fight; as, if you drive me to it, you may find, and find to you cost!

Der. The lady means mischief.—(*To* Mrs. M.) Mistress, let me ask you to bear one thing in mind:—your men are unarmed, whilst mine are armed to the teeth. I would fain avoid bloodshed; but should you work upon them, your men may chance to give us trouble. If they force us to it, we shall not scruple, in the King's affairs, to use our arms. So there, I warn you.

Will. Mother, desist:—there's blood enough to my account already.

Mrs. M. Hush!—(*To* Der.) You waste your words. If blood be shed, be it upon your own head!—Do you think I love war and its horrors more than you? Not I; but my case is desperate; war is my last resource; and therefore, I welcome war.—Now hearken to me. My men will fight to the last. They are unarmed, you say:—but, recollect, in a house like this there can be no lack of firearms; and should these be short, they shall take scythes and mow you down, axes and cleave your skulls, bills, choppers, and reaping-hooks,—and these make hideous weapons . . . You were best have a care! you've roused me;—I am desperate. I have it in my power to make this Christmas Eve one that shall be told of long after you and I are in our graves; that shall be fatal to hundreds, and bitter to the babe unborn.

—So, officer, take your choice. You say you would avoid bloodshed : if you mean what you say, give me your word to let my son pass free and leave the country ; and bloodshed shall be avoided. But refuse ; and, sooner than see him dragged from before my eyes to the gallows, I 'll see the ground strewn with corpses, the gutters run with blood, the virgin mantle of the earth, the new-fall'n snow, grow as red as sin, and not a man left alive to tell the tale to-morrow ! Take your choice.

Lobb. I 've waited while you said your say, mis'ess ; —now hear you mine. Outside yonder window just now, I had time to catch a glimpse of these same stout fellows you speak of ;—and what do you think I saw ? I saw them run, one behind the other, across the yard— leaping and capering like mad things. And as I entered the room, I saw them run, one behind the other, into the barn—for all the world like rats into the trap. And no sooner were they safe inside, than some of our men shut the door upon 'em . . .

Mrs. M. Ah . . . !

Lobb. Fastened it, and mounted guard. So that your boasted forces are at this moment eating their hearts out in the dark ;—and, without they burn the barn down, there they stay until we choose to let 'em out !—So much for your fighting-men.

Isa. For shame ! Oh, how brave, how clever you can show yourselves against one defenceless man !

Mrs. M. Then all is lost indeed. [*Her manner has undergone another change.*]

Der. And now we must be getting under way . . .

Lobb. 'Tis high time.

Mrs. M. All's lost; all's lost! Haul down the flag . . . throw up the sponge! and, Coastguard, when you leave this house, you may point to it when you please, and tell the passer-by that there dwells a woman who since she was told that her son must die a shameful death has never smiled again . . . d'you hear me? never smiled again. (*To* WILL.) My son, good-bye. Let me fold you to my heart once more. (*Embracing him.*) Willie . . . ! good-bye.—And the rest o' you, 'give ye good night.—(*As she goes out.*) My heart is broke.

[*Exit* R.]

Will. Follow her, Isabel.

Isa. Don't ask it . . . I will stay with you to the last.

Will. Playfair . . .

[*Exit* PLAY. *after* MRS. M.]

Der. (*to himself*). I'm a poor man; but I'd give my share o' the Gover'ment Reward, and summat besides, to leave this job alone! I do not like it.

Lobb (*to* WILL). Are you ready?

Will. Ready.

[*As he silently takes a last leave of* ISABEL, *the locked door of the Supper-room is tried from the outside.*]

Der. Ha!

Jack (*without*). Open the door there, I say! who has fastened the door? [*He beats upon it.*]

Lobb (*to* DER.). Can the prisoners in the barn have got free?

Der. Ay; tis they, sure enough!

Isa. Then there's hope for us yet!

Jack (*without*). Will you open the door there, I say?

Lobb (*seizing* WILL *by the collar*). Come! we've tarried too long . . .

Jack (*without*). You won't open it . . . ? Then . . . here goes!

[*He breaks in the door, and appears in the doorway.*]

Isa. (*overjoyed*). The faithful Jack!—Oh, you're a friend indeed . . . you can help us!

Jack. Ay, and will!—(*To the Officers.*) Avast there, ye cowardly swabs! did ye think to keep Jack in by turning the key . . . ?

Der. There's only one of 'em after all.

Lobb. Another of the smuggling gentry;—I know his face.—(*To* JACK.) This way, my bully-boy . . . !

Jack. You're too kind;—you are indeed!

[*As* LOBB *tries to close with him,* JACK *knocks him down.*]

Lobb. Ugh! [*He lies stunned.*]

Isa. Well done, Jack !

Jack. Hurrah, skipper ! never say die.

Der. (*shouting to his men*). Ho, shipmates, a-hoy !
[*He blows his bo'sun's whistle.*]

Jack. Ah, would ye . . . ?　[*Grapples with* Der.]

Isa. (*springing to door* C.) There are more of them
outside, Jack :—*this* shall keep them there ! [*She bars
the door.*]

Jack (*struggling with* Der.).　That's my clever
girl . . . !

Isa. (*to* Will.). Now fly, Will ! fly for your life !

Der. (*struggling*). Ho! shipmates, I say . . . a
rescue !　Beat in the door.

　　[*Coastguardsmen without thunder upon door* C,
　　　　endeavouring to force an entrance.]

Jack. Now, Will; now's your time ! look alive . . .
I can't hold un long.

Isa. And the door must give way immediately !　You
have not a moment to lose . . . fly, fly for your life !

Will. Then, farewell, Isabel ; farewell for evermore . . . !—The dead man who returns to his friends
does wrong.

　　　　　　[*Exit* Will. L.]

Der. (*struggling with* Jack, *and shouting*). Ho, shipmates ! beat it in, beat it in . . . a rescue, I say ; a
rescue !

[*The Coastguardsmen without continue to thunder on the door.*]

Will. (without). Jack !

Jack (starting). Eh ?

[*He relaxes his grasp of* DERRICK, *who, seizing the advantage, throws him and springs forward to un-bar door* C *and admit his men.*]

Isa. (supplicating). O sir ! for pity's sake . . .

Der. (roughly). Stand aside.

[*He removes the bar ;—*ISA. *hides her face.*]

Der. (partly opening the door, and addressing the men outside.) All right, my lads !—for the present, *stay where you are.* .

[*He closes door.*]

Isa. (scarce believing her senses). What . . . ? You have saved him !

Der. Say no more, Miss. After all, there 's One that 's above the King : may He pardon the breach of duty !

Jack (coming forward). Give us your hand, sir. *You* a Revenue Officer !—you was meant for better things : you 'd ha' made a smuggler . . . one of a thousand !

Will. (without). Jack !

Der. (to JACK). Follow your captain, man.

Jack. Then good-bye, all !

Old H. (rising and coming forward). Son Jack, son Jack . . . ! time up, eh ?

H

Jack. Time 's up, father.

Old H. Then farewell, fare-'ee-well, boy ; God be wi'
ye !—I doubt 'twill be a long, long day or I see your
face again.

Jack. Perhaps it may : that 's more than we can tell :
—that 's what friends who part as we' be parting can never
tell.—Hows'ever, if our spell at home 's been short, it
has been sweet . . . Cheer up ! Prue shall be good to
ye ;—and I 'll hope to greet ye, at some happier time,
with a ' Messmate, ho ! what cheer ? '

Will. (without). Jack !

Jack. Ay, ay ! (*To* Isa.) Good-bye, my heart ; may
fair weather be your portion on the cruise of life . . .
God bless you ! God bless you all . . . good-bye, good-
bye, good-bye !

[*Exit* Jack.   *A pause.*]

Der. (*to* Isa.). They have still to pass our sentry at
the door ;—but they 're two to one ; they 'll do it, if they
keep their wits about them.—Listen ! do ye hear aught ?

Isa. Nothing . . . nothing but the crowing of a cock.

Der. That should announce the dawn ;—but the day
breaks languidly at this season.—Once outside the
house, the twilight will stand them in good stead.

Lobb (*beginning to recover consciousness*). Eh . . . .
Derrick, I say . . . hold him ! (*Sitting up.*) Eh . . . ?
why, where 's the prisoner ?

Der. Gone !

Lobb. Gone . . . ! You 've never let him slip through your fingers ?

Der. I say he 's gone.

Lobb. Gone . . . ? Which way ?

Der. Through that door.

Lobb. Then he can't be gone far.

[*Exit* LOBB L.]

Der. By this time they ought to be clear. (*Opening door* C *and speaking through it.*) My lads, you may come in.

[*Enter a Detachment of Coastguardsmen.*]

Der. Well, mates ! our man has giv'n us the slip after all ;—but, as Lobb says, he can't be gone far.

[*Re-enter* LOBB.]

Well ?

Lobb. Damnation . . . ! he 's gone indeed.

Der. But our sentry . . . ?

Lobb. Asleep at his post !

Isa. Thank God !

Lobb. Thank our own cursed blundering !

Der. (*to* LOBB). Give chase, eh ?

Lobb. Give chase ? when he 's got the start of us, and his knowledge o' the country worth all ours put together ! Better go home and to bed, say I ;—that 's the fittest place for us. We are made fools of here.

Der. I believe you are right.—Fall in, men.—(*To* Isa.) Good night, young lady—(*under his breath*) remember, *silence.*—(*To his Men.*) Right turn . . . by the right . . .

[*Exeunt* Derrick, Lobb, *and Coastguardsmen.*]

Isa. Now to let his mother know that he is safe !

[*Exit* Isa.]

Sol. (*coming out from his concealment*). I suppose that is the end.

[*Enter* Davy, Hobnail, Swingtree, Tucker, Timothy, Nick, *and the other Guests.*]

Davy. Whew . . . ! what a relief to get a breath of air once more.

Hob. And to behold a light !

Swing. And to feel the warmth o' a good coal fire . . .

Tim. After bein' stifled, an' starved, and frighted out o' our wits !

Tuck. Frighted ! I believe ye, neighbour.—I should never ha' believed as 'twere possible for a man to see so much i' the dark ;—and I thank my good genus 'a did not come to me when I was alone !

Nick. (*fearfully*). And what might 'a be like, Goodman Tucker ? for, for my part, I kep' my eyes shut.— 'A had horns, had 'a ?

Tuck. Ay, had 'a ;—horns and a tail.

Nick. God bless us !

[*Enter* PRUDENCE.]

Prue. A scurvy trick to play on decent folks—a scurvy trick, I say ! Just let me come across the ill-bred, good-for-nothing scamp who fastened the door . . . just let me come across him, that's all !

Davy. Now who could it ha' been, Mis'ess Hicka-thrift ?

Prue. I'd give money, I would, to know !

[*Enter* CUTHBERT.]

Cuth. Then I can tell you. I know who let us out ; and he it was who shut us in.—It was one of the Coast-guard.

All. The Coastguard !

Cuth. The Coastguard have paid Windy Walls a visit to-night.—You all remember the price offered for my brother's capture ? that brought them here ;—and they wanted us out of the way while they did their work. The barn-door was opened by a man left behind for the purpose ; and, though he would answer no questions, I saw at once how the whole thing had happened.

Swing. Did you ever hear the like !

Cuth. I fear they have carried Will off with them.

Guests. Poor chap !

Cuth. Ah . . . ! 'twill go hardly with him.

Hob. That it will.

Prue. If so be they have taken Will, they have taken my good-man too ;—for where one goes, t' other follows. —O my poor Jack ! he would climb out at the roof at the risk o"s neck, and now 'a 's gone from the frying-pan into the fire indeed.

Hob. 'Tis a cruel night's work.

Sol. (*aside*). Haw, haw !

Cuth. (*to himself*). My friend Solomon . . . ! The force of art must yet further go.—(*Aloud, imperatively.*) Let no one leave the kitchen.—Friends, a dark suspicion rises on my mind ;—there 's a traitor in the camp !

Guests. A traitor !

Cuth. It must be so. Without information laid by one of us here to-night, how could the Coastguard have got wind of Will's return ?

Sol. (*aside*). Eh?

Cuth. I ask you, how ?

Hob. I 'm clean dumfounded.

Sol. (*aside*). What is he up to now ?

Davy. Is there any one you suspect, master ?

Cuth. No one.—There 's not a man here present, I believe, but has reason to be grateful to my family ; and I know not where to look for a villain so black-hearted that he could repay our kindness with a piece of work like this.

Swing. If such there be, hanging 's too good for un.

Cuth. By Heaven it is! let me but once lay hand upon him, and if there's a bone left whole in his body . . .

Sol. Ugh, ugh! [*He attempts to slip out.*]

Davy (*intercepting him*). Where away now, Sol?

Tim. Why, you be all of a shake.

Far. And hark how's teeth be chattering!

Cuth. What's that?—(*To* DAVY.) Bring him here.— Now, tell me the truth, Sol;—where have you been to-night?

Sol. (*boldly*). If you please, Maister Cuthbert, I've never been outside t' door.

Cuth. I'm glad of it . . . but are you *sure* of that?

Sol. Certain sure.

Cuth. (*sternly*). Then your shoes belie you, sir;—for those are the shoes of a man who has crossed country. How come they in that state;—answer me?

Davy. Ay, answer that if ye can.

Hob. (*to the bystanders*). This do look black against un.

Swing. Why, his face is the pictur' o' guilt.

Tuck. I'd my suspicions fro' the first!

Cuth. Now, Sol, I wait your answer.

Sol. (*changing his note*). Oh, . . . ! they be all against me, every one!

Cuth. Not at all! Tell us frankly, like an honest lad, what errand took ye abroad on such a night as this, and not a hair of your head will we harm.—But if you won't speak freely, we shall have to try if we can't make you.

Sol. Oh, what shall I do . . . ? (*Wringing his hands.*) O Maister! dont'ee be hard on a pore boy . . . indeed I didn't go for to do it . . . indeed I didn't know what were to come o't . . . indeed I 'll never do the like again . . . !

Davy. D' ye hear *that?* he owns to it.

Guests. Who would ha' believed it!

Hob. Who, indeed? to think that a creetur' such as that, who from his cradle up was never no good to mortal man, should yet have it in his power to work such mischief! The ways of Providence are strange.

Cuth. I have heard that he 'd a spite against my brother . . .

Davy. Why so he had! Will set us on, one day, to toss un in a blanket . . .

Tuck. Ah! I 've heard say there 's none like a natural for cherishing a grudge.

Cuth. Then this is his revenge! [*He seizes* Sol.]

Sol. (*falling on his knees*). O Maister Cuthbert! have mercy on me . . . you know the truth . . .

Cuth. Yes; I, know the truth . . . Get up, get up! and get ye gone out of my sight. [*Flings him from him.*]

[*Exit* Sol, *running the gauntlet of the Guests.*]

Cuth. (*to himself*). My schemes are crowned . . .

O Isabel! there have been women won by many a dark deed, but never one so dearly bought as you.

[*Enter* PLAYFAIR.]

Play. Prudence, Prudence! to your mistress.

[*Exit* PRUE.]

Cuth. What's the matter?

Play. Oh, enough's the matter, master;—but what the matter is it passes me to tell.

Cuth. Explain.

Play. When my mistress beheld your brother i' the hands of Justice, she begged and prayed for him, that it might ha' melted a heart of stone to hear her prayers. But the Officers was deaf to them all. And when she saw them about to bear him away, she took her leave of him and went out, saying that her heart was broke. And by Will's bidding I went with her. And when she was come to her own room, she sat for a long while silent;— and for heaviness of heart and fear of crossing her, I also held my peace. And then, all at once, to my amazement, she set to and fell a-laughing . . . but, what a laugh it was! a thousand times rather would I have heard her cry. Well, she laughed long; and then, just as suddenly as she had begun, she ceased, and turned to me, and says she, 'What was I laughing at?' I was taken aback like, and replied, ''Deed, mistress, that's more than I can tell ye!' and says she then,

H *

'You're an old fool!' and with that fell to laughing again.

[*Enter* ISA.]

Cuth. Isabella, your news?

Isa. O Cuthbert! I know not what to say; but I am full of fears.

Cuth. What do you fear?

Isa. Listen, and but too surely you will guess.—I found your mother laughing—laughing so long and loud that it was terrible to hear. 'Aunt!' said I, 'for God's sake don't laugh like that.' Whereupon she wept.

Cuth. Did not tears bring relief?

Isa. No, no! presently she began to sing . . .

Cuth. To sing!

Isa. Yes; and sang snatches of the songs of her old happy days, both sad and gay;—but, on her lips, the gayest were the saddest.

Cuth. What next?

Isa. Oh, then she said her prayers;—and then, seizing the opportunity, I coaxed her and put her to bed —for she's as gentle as a lamb. But she will not sleep. She sits up in the bed and never ceases talking—first of one thing, then of another.—When I left her she had somehow got it into her poor head that she had a journey to go . . . 'But 'tis late an' cold,' she said, 'I doubt we shall scarce ha' light enough left to see the way.'—And then, answering herself, 'Well! we must grope for it, then :—for what must be, must . . . Or how would it be to hunt for glow-worms and stick 'em in our hats, as pitmen use with candles. We should be gallantly lighted on our way, methinks ; and might march along boldly enow !'—I fancy that her wandering wits had travelled back to old times.

Cuth. I see how it is.—The events of the night have proved too much for her ;—her mind has failed.

Play. Poor Mistress ! well, she has found a refuge at last from all her troubles.

Hob. But what a refuge ! alack the day !

Isa. Yet all might still be well if I could but get her to understand that Will is safe.

Cuth.
Guests. } *Safe !*

Isa. Yes, safe :—in my distress for my aunt I had forgot to tell you.

Cuth. But how . . . ?

Isa. Indeed I can hardly tell . . .—(*To herself.*) Before so many strangers, I must not forget the Officer's caution !—(*Aloud.*) It all happened like a dream ; and I only know that at the very moment when he was about to be led off a prisoner, almost by a miracle (as it seemed) Will got safe away, and 'Jack with him.—Their departure was as sudden and unexpected as had been their return.

Cuth. Then William will come back?

Isa. No, Cuthbert.   As he went out, he bade me fare-well for ever;—and my heart tells me that we shall not see him again.

> [ISA. *and* CUTH. *go up stage :—the rest gather to the front.*]

Play. 'Twas strange that they should come back to-night, of all nights i' the year,—just when we had been talking of them.

Swing. Just what I had been thinking myself.

Tuck. Well, gossip . . . ? did not your thoughts recall anything pertick'lar to your mind?

Swing. Faith! that they did.

Hob. Let us hear what it was?

Swing. (*in spite of himself*). The old man's words o' last night.

Play. Why, what words do ye mean?

Swing. (*with evident reluctance*). That, on Christmas Eve . . .

Davy. (*taking the words out of his mouth*). . . . the cock crows all night long . . .

Tuck. And the bees i' the hives sing hymns o' praise . . .

Hob. And the cattle in stall fall down on their knees to worship . . .

Tim. And the Powers of Darkness . . .

Far. . . . for a while forego their sway . . .

Davy. And the dead put on their earthly shapes once more, and return to their homes . . .

Play. (God A'mighty bless us!)

Davy. To dine and dance wi' the living!

Guests. To dine and dance wi' the living!

Isa. (*to* CUTH.). Cuthbert! do you hear them?

Cuth. I hear.

Play. God A'mighty bless us . . . !—Miss Isabella! you was in the room when the Master and Jack took leave ;—tell me—I've my reasons for askin' ye—did you happen to notice the hour?

Isa. I did not . . . yet stay . . . I did.—Jack was the last to go; and as he went out, I heard the cock crow :—it was day-break.

Play. (*with emphasis*).—*But at cock-crow, when the morning breaks, they return to whence they came !*

[*The Guests are silent.*]

Old H. (*waking out of a doze, and rising*). Well, well! I must be bidding ye good night, neighbours. Time flies ; the best o' friends must part . . . and these be late hours for a man o' my years.

Play. Stay . . .

Old H. By your leave . . .

Play. (*detaining him*). Stay . . .! Daddy, you told us last night that you should see your son . . .

Old H. Well! see en I did.

Play. You did. What does it mean . . . ?—Shall we see him, shall we see the Master, again?

Old H. There! now ye ask more than I can tell ye.

Play. (*persisting*). What do you think?

Old H. (*peevishly*). Ay, ay . . . it matters little what an old man like me may think.

Play. But whither, think you then, are they bound?

Old H. Where neither you nor I would follow.

Play. To begin a new life, under a new law, in the New World . . . perhaps?

Old H. Who can tell . . . ? to begin a new life, under a new law, in the New World . . . perhaps! Well, well! I told ye I should see un to-night, and see un I did . . . But, Lord help us! these be late hours for a man o' my years. By your leave, steward; by your good leave. I wish ye a good night . . . but, nay!—for yonder is the peep o' day . . . I wish ye a 'Good-morning!'

[*Exit.*]

Davy. (*breaking the silence of the Guests*). Bear me witness, all of ye! You heard me laugh at that old man last night . . . if I live to be a hundred, s' help me, I 'll never laugh at the like again.—May I come to a bad end if I do!

[*He bursts into tears.*]

Play. You are right there.—Who can tell but the

thoughts of Old Age, on the brink o' the grave, may be longer thoughts than ours?

Isa. O Cuthbert! your brother's words come back to me now with new meaning . . .

Cuth. What did he say?

Isa. He spoke of death and of the land beyond the grave, as never man spoke of them before.

Play. (*solemnly*). These facts are stranger than the strangest fancies ever I heard.

Hob. The ways of Providence are strange, neighbour;—and 'tis not for simple men, the likes of us, to fathom them.

Play. That is true . . .—(*Addressing the Guests.*) And now, good folks, 'tis time for us to separate. Little did we think, when we came together last night, what was to befall ere we should part. It has pleased Heaven to visit this house heavily: our good mistress is stricken; our Master . . . but, for the rest of what has taken place, I cannot speak out all that's in my mind; only this I think, that the youngest among us will remember it to his dying day.—And now let each man go soberly and decently to his own house, and there lay to heart what we have seen.

Hob. So be it;—'wish ye good night.

Swing. Good night!

Cuth. (*coming forward as the Guests are about to depart*). Stay . . . one word before you go. (*To* ISA., *gaily, taking her by the hand.*) Cousin, a boon! Since William will not return, the sole obstacle to our union is removed :—grant me the happiness, ere they separate, of presenting you to these humble well-wishers as my affianced bride.

Isa. (drawing back). Cuthbert! What, can you talk of marriage at a moment such as this . . . ? Yet, since you've broached it, I've a word to say on that subject you may as well hear now as to-morrow.—Last night you spoke to me of love, and I did not silence you . . . but last night I was a different woman.—Last night I was a vain and thoughtless girl;—but I tell you that the knowledge and wisdom which to others come with years have to me come in a single night.—Henceforward, speak no more to me of love. Henceforth I am no maiden free to hear you ; but your brother's widow, vowed to tears and to his memory.

Cuth. Isabella . . . !

Isa. These are no idle words. The same blood runs in these veins as in your own, as in your mother's ; remember that. We are a race apart—you know it ;— and when one of us has spoken as I now speak, we depart not from our word.

Cuth. Isabella . . .

Isa. Enough.

Cuth. Enough, then ;—you shall have your way.—But, if you will not hear me speak of love, you shall at least hear who the man is you reject; how he has shown his love for you . . .—(*Wildly.*) 'Tis truth, whom Fate will destroy she first drives mad!—(*To the Guests.*) Hear, all of you! you have heard much to-night already; well, the best o' the tale's to tell.—Hear me, all of you, I say! and henceforward, in the foremost rank among the Heroes and Giants of Iniquity, set the name of Cuthbert Mar!

Isa. (*in her turn dismayed*). Cuthbert!

Cuth. Call me not Cuthbert! Call me Judas—call me Cain. Cain slew his brother; Judas betrayed his Master;—but who betrayed my brother . . . ? [*Silence.*] It was I! [*The Guests start back amazed, but incredulous.*] Consider: who had so much to gain by the act as I? By Will's return I lost fortune, fame, and love: by his destruction all might be retrieved. I was born for intrigue. I worked upon the base mind of that idiot boy; I sped him on his midnight journey. When he returned, fearing your interference, I devised a trap and led you into it. And, to put the cope on my performance, I made a scapegoat of my accomplice.

Guests (*as the truth breaks upon them, appalled*). Oh, horrible . . . !

Cuth. Horrible; yet true.—(*To* ISA.) And all this I did for love of you. For love of riches . . . ? Never! for riches now are mine, but I fling them to the winds . . . for love of you.—(*Softening.*) O Isabel! has any

I

man done more than this?   Others have given their
lives for the love of woman—but I have given my soul !
The hand of Heaven itself is seen against me ; I am
caught in my own toils.

Isa. (*recoiling*). Oh, horrible . . . !

Cuth. Beloved . . . farewell !   Dearest, most beautiful . . . and you loved me for one hour.   But your
love was cold: my father was from Spain—and oh ! if
you had loved as I loved you, you would have loved me
still :—you would have clung to me, though the hand that
grasped your own hand had been red, even as my soul
in truth is black, with the guilt of a brother's murder ;—
you would have followed me now, though the snow had
been our marriage-bed, and the light that lighted us to
it the cold light of those dying stars !—Farewell ! be
happy.—And, friends all, farewell !—friends of a summer
day.   Farewell ! I say, and again farewell ! a long farewell . . . for you shall see my face no more !

[*As he goes out, the*

CURTAIN FALLS.

L'ENVOI.

A STORM-TOSS'D sailor in a sinking ship,
   Remembering friends and home, these lines I scrawl;
Whilst, with undaunted brow and unblanch'd lip,
   My comrades, idle, wait the end of all.
And now the bottle . . . . Ha! boon friend of yore,
You have served me often—serve me yet once more.

Now, o'er the rolling waters ride at ease:
Pass from these tempests to serener seas:
Stay not for drifting seaweed, or isle of birds
(Regardful always of the intrusted words),
But seek a harbour in some pebbly cove,
Where kindly creatures dwell with neighbours' love;
There find a friend—and bring him safe from me
This Message launch'd on the Eternal Sea!

POEMS.

EVENING.—AN ECLOGUE.

Ἕσπερε, πάντα φέρεις, ὅσα φαινόλις ἐσκέδασ' αὔως,
φέρεις ὄϊν, φέρεις αἶγα, φέρεις ματέρι παῖδα.

SAPPHO'S Fragments.

First Shepherd—

 Now day draws to its close : the Sun
 Droops in the west, his journey done . . .

Second Shepherd—

 And, duly, from her mansion fair—
 Intent on charitable care—
 Bounteous, benign, of matchless worth,
 The gracious lady, Eve, comes forth ;

First Shepherd—

 Upon whose head the kneeling clown
 Prays, as she goes, a blessing down.

Second Shepherd—

 Ay ;—'tis her wish'd-for coming brings
 Sweet respite to all labouring things :

First Shepherd—

 'Tis she whose hand, with loving care,
 Lightens the burden all things bear . . .

Second Shepherd—

 And soothes each poor noon-fever'd brow—
 While murmuring comfort sweet and low—
 With gentle touch and cool.

First Shepherd—

　　　　　　　　　　　'Tis she,
　　Who, like a parent, tenderly—
　　Gathering once more, as at the first,
　　Whate'er the exuberant dawn dispers'd—
　　By starlight, through the purple gloam,
　　Leads all live things, her children, home!

Second Shepherd—

　　She brings what, whilst the morn was grey,
　　Heav'nward, with music, took its way,
　　To range the air—with weary wings,
　　The bird back to its nest she brings.

First Shepherd—

　　Back to their fold she brings the flocks:

Second Shepherd—

　　Back from the field the toiling ox:

First Shepherd—

　　Back to their caves all creatures wild:

Second Shepherd—

　　Me back, once more, to wife and child!

First Shepherd—

　　Dearer than morn, or night, or noon,
　　To shepherd, Evening, is thy boon:

Second Shepherd—

　　Than moon by night, or sun by day,
　　Fairer, O Star of Eve, thy ray!

SPRING, SONG, AND SOLITUDE.

I.

THE Spring returns: the Earth grows young—
 Grows young as never man shall grow—
And cries, with many a silvery tongue,
 As loud and clear as long ago.

The world is green: in every vein
 New life with new-born gladness thrills:
The light of Youth is found again!
 Hear and rejoice, ye patriarch hills!

II.

The woodland bird, when Spring returns,
 Pours all its gladness on the air;
And sings the joys the loved one earns—
 Sings that the earth is green and fair:

And would that I, like thee, sweet bird,
 Might set my joys, my sadness free,
Singing—uncared for and unheard—
 A song that's all too hard for me!

I *

III.

Oh, in this fair far-off retreat,
   At patient Evening's peaceful hour,
As our first father met, to meet—
   Where shades are deep, in brake or bower—

Some form of female loveliness,
   As white as if a moonbeam fell—
Come from another world to bless,
   And evermore with me to dwell!

A NIGHT-PIECE.

WHEN saner men are sound a-bed,
　And beasts in woods and fields are still,
The lonely paths alone I tread,
　And wander on o'er dale and hill:

O'er waste and woodland, ford and fence,
　My onward course uncheck'd I steer,
Unseen—as walks the Pestilence,
　When damps infect the sorrowing year.

The screech-owl from her touchwood house
　Peeps forth, and chides me as I go,
That thus her fretful chicks I rouse
　And through the echoing woods halloo.

For no latch clicks; no footstep beats
　In tune to mine the loud highway,
Save his, whose face the night secretes—
　Whose craft abhors the eyes of day.

What goal have I to gain to-night?
　Yon haunted tower, or yonder hill,
Which, on the utmost verge of sight,
　Cuts clear into the twilight still?

Not these : a friendlier bourn I know,
    Five furlongs from the neighbouring town,
Where, o'er the broad champaign below,
    A bench-encircled beech looks down :—

A pleasant haunt when eves are long,
    And mild, and full of balm, in May ;
When wordy elders round it throng,
    And children with the beech-mast play ;

And lovers, lingering on till night—
    Still whispering with the still-whispering leaves—
Score on its bark the troth they plight,
    And many a trust the tree receives :

A pleasant spot when ponderers see
    The sweet old tale retold once more,
Mature Content and infant Glee—
    The simple life-play acted o'er.

But now—when Life is laid to sleep,
    And its unlantern'd watchman I ;
Who hear alone the wheezing sheep,
    And, far away, the wild-duck's cry—

Now smiles with more congenial air
    Forsaken seat and sombre tree ;
Which smiled, with light and laughter there,
    For all the world but not for me.

The hour is mine :—on couch or straw,
    The scheming active myriads lie—
Clownish contempt with kingly awe,
    Like garments, for the time laid by.

The hour is mine. A charmer's lands,
    The finger'd branches o'er me pass;
Whilst, rustling, in the woods expands
    The Spring's new life in leaves and grass;

Till Sleep, from dreamland's confines pale—
    That lazy lover of soft sound—
Floats on the hawthorn-incensed gale,
    And weighs me, nerveless, to the ground;

With silk-smooth arms about my neck,
    And cozening whispers in my ear—
As idle as the chattering beck,
    Which none but dreamers pause to hear;—

Till, as from some insidious cup,
    Inspired forbidden powers to wield,
Strange phantoms could I conjure up
    To move and mime in yon grey field.

Behold! the shades of all those lives
    That fill'd the evening air with noise—
Grave husbands with their mild-faced wives,
    And grandsires crook'd, and girls and boys;

Striplings and maidens, hand in hand,
　　And babes—our life's small sweet spring flowers—
Like strangers—in a far-off land
　　Mindful of home and bygone hours—

Come back once more ;—and, one by one,
　　With wistful mien and eyes downcast—
Weak wraiths from worlds without a sun—
　　Still silently go trooping past.

So sad to see I scarce can stay
　　For 'By your leave,' or, 'With your leave,'
To take my stand beside the way
　　And pluck the foremost by the sleeve.

'Now, gossip, whither, pray, so late?—
　　Hark! though the noon o' night be near,
Dawn yet shall burst his dungeon-gate—
　　Where Doubt stands sentinel with Fear—

'And, o'er old Ocean's labouring waste,
　　O'er silent city, stretching plain,
Charged with dear hope, enjoin'd to haste,
　　Shall ride, a messenger, amain—

'An angel—and like angels bright,
　　Arm'd with the name that all revere,
Who hark and speed him on his flight
　　To find and greet and help us here!

'When he, from yonder glimmering slope,
  Pausing his outworn steed to breathe,
Waves his plumed casque, and shouts us, " Hope !"
  Hope to the hearts that touch on death !

'Then straight, from signal-tower and hill,
  Our watchmen shall give on the cry;
Which, through the throng'd streets echoing still,
  Shall reach the hearts that faint and die ;—

'Till, with one voice, around, afar,
  Tongued like the forests, winds and waves,
Choir upon choir shall hail the Star—
  The Morning Star that speaks and saves !'

So, in the enthusiasm of my sleep,
  Moved by strong love and pity, I spake ;
When, pierced with words like flames that leap,
  I started from the ground awake !

I stood alone.—That sorrowing train
  O'er the bleak world had ta'en its way—
Ne'er on my sight to rise again,
  Though life be blest with many a day.

SONG.—YESTERDAY.

Could, oh, could I, Yesterday!
  Of thy many moments one
Snatch and hide—and hie away,
  Like thieves who with their plunder run:

Over the far hills could I fly,
  Clasping it ever to my breast;
No Caliph were so rich as I
  In Araby the Blest!

EDINBURGH UNIVERSIY PRESS:
T. & A. CONSTABLE, Printers to Her Majesty.